A TOUCH OF FATE

FATED FOR CURVES - BOOK ONE

AIDY AWARD

SAVE THE GEEK GIRL, SAVE THE WORLD

Kady Ayininkizi, your anything but average curvy geek girl, has isolated herself in her brand new tiny house in the mountains because she's tired of being bullied by the alphaholes of the world.
The spaceship that crashes in her backyard brings the first alien she's ever encountered, make that the sexiest alien, ever. When he insists she help him get to some weird place called Rogue, New York, she is determined to outwit the men in black, in spite of the growing attraction that she knows will never come to fruition.

Black Barrett can't lead his elite team of shape-shifting Star Marines on their mission to stop the scourge that is the spectral soul stealers if he can't get to
Rogue, New York.

His best bet is the luscious witch who doesn't seem to know how to use her powers but has earth's lawmen running in circles with her sexy-as-hell smarts.
But when her powers surface and bring the spectrals down around them in force, he must choose.
Save his one true love that the Fates have brought him, or save the world.

Copyright © 2017 by Aidy Award.

All rights reserved. No part of this publication may be reproduced, distributed or transmitted in any form or by any means, including photocopying, recording, or other electronic or mechanical methods, without the prior written permission of the publisher, except in the case of brief quotations embodied in critical reviews and certain other noncommercial uses permitted by copyright law.

Publisher's Note: This is a work of fiction. Names, characters, places, and incidents are a product of the author's imagination. Locales and public names are sometimes used for atmospheric purposes. Any resemblance to actual people, living or dead, or to businesses, companies, events, institutions, or locales is completely coincidental.

Cover by Melody Simmons

A Touch of Fate / Aidy Award. – 3rd ed.

INTRODUCTION

Welcome to Aidy's Alternate Universe, where Dragons don't exist... but Space Marine Bears do!

Reader: What's the deal here, Aidy?

Aidy: See... A few years ago, I wrote a series about shifters from outer space fighting for their fated mates and their souls. I loved it and it was lots of fun, but because I was a new author, not very many people read it.

I decided to re-write the whole series and turn all the heroes into Dragon Warriors in my Black Dragon Brotherhood series. But I love these space bears so I've turned their stories into an alternate universe for readers where I imagined that dragons didn't exists, but these curvy girls still needed soul mates.

Reader: Alternate universe? Kind of like in comic books, oh, like Spiderman and the Spide-Verse?

Aidy: Yep, kind of. My two alternate universes won't ever meet, that would be weird for the heroines. lol

Reader: So, it is Touch of Fate the same story as Tamed?

Aidy: Think of it like this: The heroine in each book is the same – Kady has has a similar journey in both stories. She needs a soul mate and to discover her power within. In the Black Dragon Brotherhood universe it's a Dragon Warrior and they fight the Shadow and the Cult of the Dead, based in Sumerian mythology. In the Fated For Curves alternate universe, they fight the Spectrals and Task Force Omega, based in Greek Mythology. In both universes, they discover the power of soul magic, fall in love, and get happy ever afters in Rogue, New York.

If you've read the Alpha Wolves Want Curves series, I've included the Troika wolf pack and their mates into this alternate universe. Those characters are mostly the same, but along with the psychic abilities I've given to the wolves' mates, I have them a bit of magic abilities since there are not elemental witches (because... no dragons.)

Reader: Cool. Do I need to read both books?

Aidy: I mean... I think you should. lol

If sci-fi and bear-shifters is your jam, read Fated For Curves. If you want more Dragon Warriors because you lurrved the Dragons Love Curves series and never want it to end, then read The Black Dragon Brotherhood.

If you just can't get enough curvy girls getting their happy ever afters with sexy alpha-shifters in an action adventure story – read them both!

Get Tamed on Amazon and in Kindle Unlimited

For my mom, who I learned about love and romance from in the first place.
Happy Birthday.

1

CRASH INTO ME

Too many systems in Black's shuttle were failing. The computer screamed his falling altitude until he couldn't take its whining voice any longer and smashed the interface to bits with his fist. Fates be damned he was going to crash on the little blue planet.

If he drowned before finding the spectral soldiers that had been plaguing the galaxy on this water-logged planet, he was going to beat back any Fate who even tried to take him to the afterlife with a stick.

He jabbed at the short-range communicator attached to his arm.

"Listen up, team. I'm going to attempt an emergency landing in the forested area ahead. Continue to Rogue, New York, and make contact with the Troika wolves. Finding the spectrals is still the key mission. I'll catch up as soon as I can."

He got "yes, sir" from his two brothers, a "got it" from Fed, and a grumble from Titian. That Fates-forsaken fox. "Titian, you copy?"

"Nope."

He didn't have time for Titian's bullshit. "Good. My long-range comms are out. Contact Electra and let her know I'm going down."

"Aw, fuck me," Titian sing-songed across the comms.

Black's ship bucked and took a steep dive. He punched at the keyboard of the flight control panel praying for a response, but what he got was the ship jerking him around, literally. A new warning siren blared, indicating the tailspin, but Black didn't have the time to care. He was too busy trying not to die.

Fucking hell. Join the Star Marines Elite Corps they said, it'll be epic they said.

He didn't need epic, he needed a damned lead on the spectrals and a way to defeat them. If one more family had to come to the Star Marines pleading for his help... No, he wouldn't think of those who grieved their sons and daughters, fathers and mothers now. If he lived through this day he'd vow to rescue as many as he could and avenge those he couldn't.

First, he had to survive, the bear inside of him taunted.

"Impact in fifteen seconds."

Black slammed his fist all the way through the console and could die happy knowing this particular computer voice would never again tell anyone else about their own impending doom.

Earth's enormous white clouds engulfed the ship bouncing and bumping him until his teeth rattled. It was only a few seconds until he broke through the cloud cover and saw the land below growing in the forward screen.

The miles of green trees and snow tipped mountains were so like his native planet. If the Fates ordained that he had to die anywhere but home, this would be where his soul would most be at rest.

Not that he was giving up. No way. Never. If he could just level the ship out to an angle that wasn't quite so steep he might be able to skim across the land and stop upright and alive. That is if no large structures or natural formations blocked his path. Like the side of that mountain.

Shit.

"Impact in ten—"

"Shut up you bag of dung." Hadn't he already killed the bitch? How was it that the computer voice had redundant systems, but the flight control didn't?

Black flipped the switch for his last-ditch effort, the manual steering column. He hadn't used one since he'd learned to fly as a cub and even then, he hadn't been good at it. Crashing a training shuttle ten feet above the ground and smashing a forty-ton piece of metal built for interspace travel were two different things. He unlocked the column from its position under the console and clicked it into place.

"Seven—"

He cursed the computer one last time and pulled up on the manual steering column with all his might. Years of battle and many more working the land he loved had given him more strength than most soldiers, man, bear, or anything else. He called upon the Fates to imbue him with more.

"Six—"

The ship continued in its downward spiral. His muscles strained, and he heard metal grinding against metal. A small explosion shook the back of the ship and he lost a chunk of one wing.

"Come on, baby. Come on." Maybe if he sweet talked her instead of cursing her she'd do his bidding.

"Five seconds to impact."

Sweat beaded on his brow and upper lip. "I'm giving you all I've got, baby. Gimme just a little back."

"Four—"

She leveled out by the tiniest degree. Black's muscles tremored and shook under the absolute exertion. "That's a good girl."

"Three—"

The ship skimmed the tops of a clump of dark evergreen trees, then dipped into them. The sound of breaking branches and the trunks clanging on the sides of the ship were louder than open laser fire in battle.

"Two—"

The last thought that flashed though his mind before impact wasn't that of his friends, family, or his life playing before his eyes. It was the fact that the medallion hanging over his heart glowed with the light of a whole damn galaxy worth of stars.

"One.

Fuck the Fates. His life was his own, and this was not how it would end.

Impact, impact, iiiimmmpaaaaccct."

2

FIRST CONTACT

Kady ran back into her tiny house on wheels and rummaged through the storage space under her bench seat. Damn it, she really needed to get more organized. There was barely any room to move in this two-hundred and fifty-five square foot place as it was. She and her big butt squeezed through spaces smaller than she ever expected she could. This clutter didn't help.

"Where is it, where is it?" She shoved aside a pair of jeans she thought she'd lost, a shoe box without a top filled with old Pokémon cards, a spare set of keys to her old apartment, and a half-eaten bag of hedgehog snacks, before she found what she was looking for.

"Aha." She pulled out the $19.99 telescope along with a chipped Death Star coffee mug tied to it with yarn and rushed back outside.

The view of the night sky continually awed her from up here in the outskirts of the mountain town of Estes Park. For the first time in her adult life she could see the creamy haze of the Milky Way. But that wasn't what had drawn her attention away from her Netflix marathon of STNG tonight.

She set up the tiny tripod on top of a nearby boulder and pointed the lens skyward. She bumped her glasses into the lens trying to get a good look. "Where did you go, little alien?"

A few minutes ago, she'd seen what she thought was a simple shooting star. The longer she looked, the more it moved, and not in a straight path. She searched the sky through the little eye-sight until she found the blob, burning through the sky.

"Holy guacamole."

She couldn't make out a shape, the power of the telescope simply wasn't strong enough, but whatever it was bucked like a bronco. The horse, not the football players.

"No way that's an asteroid or a comet or a weather balloon."

Something man-made...or not made by humans at all, but by aliens was falling straight to Earth and headed for her backyard.

"Sweet." She was going to make first contact. Did the Prime Directive apply to her as a pre-warp society?

She glanced back up and the bronco ball of light was a heck of a lot closer.

"Oh, shitbuckets." It was headed for her backyard. It was going to crash into the one piece of the world she owned and destroy everything.

Where were Bruce Willis, Ben Affleck and Steve Buscemi with their drilling machines and atomic bombs when a girl needed them?

The not a shooting star quickly turned into a fiery ball. A spaceship shaped one, with wings, make that wing, a hull, and giant laser gun-missile weapons array.

Great. Awesome. Alien spaceships were real.

Hell, yeah.

But they were going to kill her, or destroy everything she'd worked so hard for, so same thing.

Hell, no.

She had to do something and fast, or her tiny house and her beloved bath house were both going up in flames, not to mention Percy and herself.

No light-sabers, no magical spells, no prayers or affirmations to the universe were going to change the path of destruction aimed at her. What could she do but run?

Nothing.

So Kady ran. For about a hundred yards. A stitch hit her in the side so deep if felt like an attack of the killer seamstresses had slowed her down. She grabbed her side and tried to speed-walk. "I swear to you Universe, if you let me save my house, I'll never ask for anything again." She gasped. "This week...or next."

The fire in the sky was getting closer. Side-stitch be damned, she had to save her house. She'd worked too hard saving every penny she'd made since she was seven-years old and being shuffled to another foster family to lose everything she had now.

She jogged a few steps, walked a few, jogged a few until her tiny house on wheels came into view.

It sat in such a perfect spot. A copse of trees surrounded the back and a meadow opened up right outside of her front door. She had sun in the morning for the solar panels and shade in the afternoon to keep the house cool. It had taken a solid week to get the satellite dish for her internet connection just right.

If these aliens ruined her sanctuary, she was going to kick their butts. As soon as she learned how to use the Force, or some Krav Maga.

Although, that would require going to town and talking to people and that meant getting out of her pajamas and well, talking to people. People sucked.

People pretended to care but didn't. People abandoned her without even so much as a have a nice life in the foster care system.

Plus, also there was that whole working out thing she wasn't really into. Still, as soon as she established first contact, she'd find out if the aliens had the technology to repair her little abode with the flick of their wrists.

That is if she or any of them survived. She looked back up at the whizzing oncoming collision and gulped.

Kady picked up her pace and gasped her way to the tiny house. She threw open the front door and scanned the room. "Percy? Where are the truck keys? Percy?"

No response and no keys. "Shit, shit, shit."

She tossed throw pillows, her Xbox remote, and a R2-D2 quilt over her shoulder. Maybe they were in her comfy chair. A Cheeto, two food pellets, and three swear words later, no keys.

"Why do I do this?" If she and her tiny house survived, she swore to finally get rid of everything that didn't bring her joy and clean up her clutter once and for all. She pushed her glasses up her nose and spun around glancing at every flat surface and some bumpy ones hoping for a glimpse of her She-Ra keychain.

Nothing, nothing, nothing. Time was running out. She really didn't want to cut and run with or without Percy.

She glanced out the window, the spaceship was close enough to see with the naked eye and it lit up the meadow.

"Dear and sweet Universe. Where the fuck are my keys?"

There, on the window sill, in the plant. She-Ra, Princess of Power. "Yesss."

Percy was going to have a rough ride.

She bolted out the door, slammed and locked it behind her and jumped into the old red pick-up truck. It took her three tries to reverse into the right position to get the trailer and the hitch lined up.

She'd only done this on her own twice. Once when she picked her tiny house up from the manufacturer in Colorado Springs and again when she's hauled it up to her brand spanking new one point seven five acres of land in Larimer County.

She'd hadn't planned to leave if she could help it, and up until tonight she hadn't needed to. Damned space alien bastards.

This was not the way to start a friendly relationship.

The sound of the ship descending on her was a low rumble now. Hurry, hurry. The only thing she had to do was get this thing hitched and move out.

The rumble in the sky turned into a screech. She fiddled with the ball of the hitch, her hands fumbling in her hurry. "Come on, come on."

She glanced up at the death ship hurtling toward her. It jerked up, to the side, took a steep dive, and then it's nose aimed right for her.

The metal of the hitch clanked into place, jamming her fingers right smack dab in between. "Ouch, ow, owie, ow, ow, ow, ouch."

She yanked her purpling fingers free and sprinted to the truck cab, ramming the keys into the ignition.

Rrrr, rrrr, rrrr, rrrph. "Don't do this to me, Herbie. Start, damn you."

Rrrr, rrrr, rrrr, rrrrrrrrrrrrrrrrrrrrrrph.

The ship jumped and then fell a hundred feet straight down, screaming toward her.

Oh, crap. She wasn't going to make it. The vessel was twenty yards in front of her.

She twisted the key one more time.

Rrrr, rrrr, rrrr.

"I'll be damned if I'm going to die here and now." Kady jumped from the truck seconds before the boom of the space ship passed over head, missing her by no more than half a foot, tossing her into the sky for an aerial cartwheel.

She landed hard ten feet away and rolled another five. For once she was glad for the extra padding on her ass. The sound of the tops of the trees breaking in the path of destruction crashed, making her curl into a ball, trying to protect her head and body from the debris.

KA-BOOOOOOOOM.

Kady's stomach imploded with a drop like a thousand cannons on the fourth of July and her ears rang with the squeal of the longest, meanest train whistle. She swallowed to keep from tossing her cookies, because that would be a waste of cookies.

When she was sure nothing was coming, up she pushed herself off the ground and stumbled, falling back down with a plop.

Great googly-mooglies, she might have blown an ear drum. She couldn't hear anything but a ringing echoing off the mountains and inside her head.

Where was the spaceship?

She stood again, put her hands out to keep her balance and found her sea legs. Luckily, her glasses had stayed on her face during all that and she could see a clear path of eviscerated ground and trees pointed toward the highway. But somehow, miraculously, thank you Universe, the ship had missed her tiny house, her truck, and twenty yards into the trees, her bath house.

Kady thrust her fist into the air. "Heck, yeah."

And she fell on her ass again. A couple of presses to her ears helped a little bit, so she tried again, holding a finger in one ear, which seemed to work.

"Holy crap on a cracker." She could see the ship, and there was something or someone, yes, a man, glowing and lying on the ground next to it.

A golden man. Not gold like he'd been tanning in the sun, and not like an Academy Award, but gold like he'd been planning on going clubbing and put on every bottle of sparkly bronzer from Walmart's clearance section.

Could she, should she get closer? See if he was breathing?

She should get in Herbie Husker and drive far, far, far

away from here. Maybe set up shop in the deserts of New York. Surely, no one would bother her there.

But he was an alien and he could be dying.

On the other hand, he and his spaceship almost killed her and everything that was dear to her.

This was a chance at first contact with an alien race.

She shook her head. What, was this, Star Trek? She was no Uhura, T'Pol, or Captain Janeway.

The authorities would be coming any minute. They would take care of everything.

Men who thought they were in charge would come marching up her side of the mountain. Authority types were the worst of the alphaholes in the world in her experience. They never understood her. Better if she bolted now.

She opened the door to Herbie, stared at it, and slammed it shut.

Damn it. She couldn't leave a possibly dying alien man lying in her backyard. He could be suffering and if he wasn't now, the sound of those sirens coming up the mountain meant he would be soon.

They'd put him under a microscope and never let him go. People were bastards, that she knew.

If she could save another being in the universe from being poked, prodded, bullied, and hurt, then she would.

It would add to her karma bank and maybe someday be returned. Not that it ever had before. No one had ever saved her.

She couldn't allow that to happen to another being.

Okay. Save the alien, save the world.

Kady glanced in the direction the emergency services

were coming from and then into the burning trees. She didn't have much time. It might work if the alien or aliens were conscious. Which would be a miracle.

She grabbed the flashlight from Herbie and headed into the hole in the trees.

"Please be a nice alien species here for first contact and not the point man in the alien invasion, because I don't know any fighter pilots that look like Will Smith."

The alien man groaned, or maybe growled. Oops. Had he heard that? Was he awake?

Another twenty yards and she could see him head to toe. And what a hell of a head, and toes, and muscled legs, and wide shoulders, holy cannolis, look at those abs.

If all aliens were built like this guy she volunteered to be Earth's ambassador to his planet. Although she wouldn't get any ambassadoring done because she'd be daydreaming all day and every night about all the dirty fun things she could do with a man like that.

Not that he'd be interested in her, but a girl could fantasize all she wanted.

He groan-growled again and one leg moved revealing more skin through the tears in his clothes. Plus, she swore she saw black fur.

Huh. A humanoid with body fur was plausible. Or maybe he just hadn't manscaped properly.

She shined the flashlight across his body, mostly to figure out what his injuries might be and to see if she could figure out how to move him, and a little bit to see more of his, uh, fur.

Her light caught on some sort of pendant hanging from

his neck. The cord was torn and ready to fall off. The stone looked like a large piece of amber, carved with a bear paw print.

A siren echoed off the mountain. They were getting closer.

No way she could help by standing here gawking at him. She took several tentative steps, and with each one, the medallion's light grew brighter. Hopefully that was a good sign, like E.T.'s heart light.

"Hello? Hello? Mr. Hotty Alien Fur Man. Can you hear me?"

3

A BEAR IN THE WOODS

A female voice penetrated Black's brain. That damned computer better shut up.

He forced one eye open, shut it again against the piercing light, took a breath that hurt to his claws and tried again. He opened his eyes, blinked and found the most beautiful girl creature he'd ever seen standing over him. No, she wasn't a girl. This was a woman. If his head would quit pounding for one damn second, he'd do his best to woo her straight into his bed.

Unless, she was a Fate come to take his soul across to the afterlife. Then she could go fuck herself. He'd stay and watch.

"Oh good, you're not dead. Well, not yet, anyway."

A Fate wouldn't ask such a question, would she? No. So, not a harbinger to the next life, that meant she was a luscious, warm, slightly out of focus, but gorgeous none-the-less, woman.

"Can you move? Oh, maybe you shouldn't move. Wait

one minute while I go see if I have a neck brace. I took CPR in the eighth grade."

"No. Do not go." This language felt thick coming off his tongue. His translator must have gotten shaken up in the crash along with the rest of his brains.

"Okay." She squatted down beside him.

If his arms didn't feel so limp and heavy he would have grabbed those luscious hips and pulled her on top of him.

Whoa. While he was as horny as the next bear, now was the not the time or place to have sex on the brain.

"I'm Kady. Can you tell me your name?"

"What's a K-D?" Maybe more than the translator implant in his brain was broken. What's a K-D? Such fool things hadn't come out of his mouth since he'd gone through the change from cub to bear and received his Soul Ember.

She laughed, and it felt like sunshine and the strongest dark liquor all rolled into one. Both his head and his cock wanted to hear more.

"I'm a Kady. I mean, that's my name. I'm a human."

Of course she was. This was Earth, the small blue planet it had taken him more time than he could afford for him and his team to get to. He blinked trying to force his brain to work.

His team. He was here to find a way to defeat the spectrals. Not to find a woman.

Well, he'd found one, and she was going home with him and straight into his bed if he had anything to say about it.

Fates above, he could hardly wait to sink his cock into her soft flesh.

No. He didn't have time for that sort of pleasure. He had a war to win.

"My name is Black—"

A shrill sound, much like his warning signals on the ship blared rhythmically from somewhere nearby.

Kady glanced over her shoulder, through the destruction his ship had caused. "Ah crap. They're coming."

"Who?"

"The men in black, the CIA, the alien abductees, take your pick. But whoever it is, won't be good."

Electra had warned him the people of this planet were primitive and under no circumstances should his team allow themselves known to anyone besides the residents of Rogue.

This mission had clusterfuck written all over it. There was too much at stake to let the people of Earth interfere. His bear wavered at the edge of shifting, ready to heal his wounds and take control.

It waited, not wanting to scare the woman away.

"I will fight them off, defend you." Just as soon as he could stand.

"Yeah, I don't think so. Can you get up? Maybe lean on me and we can hide you in my house until the hubbub is over. Although, you might crush me. Geez, your big." She covered her mouth with both hands. "Oops, sorry. I did not mean to say that out loud. But seriously, if you don't want to be experimented on and anally probed, we've got to get a move on."

"Anally probed?" What sort of people were these Earthers?

"Oh, wait. That's what the aliens do. If I take you in, you

have to promise not to put anything near my anus." She wagged her finger at him.

"I promise not to put anything near your luscious ass unless you ask me to." He blinked and swallowed. How had that popped out of his mouth?

"That will have to do. Come on." She laced one arm around his torso and helped him to his feet. "Oomph. You are not going to fit in my front door."

Her touch scorched his skin, burning up his arm across his chest where her body was pressed to his side and straight to his heart. His bear side roared out its claim on her. Black wanted to both jump away and hold her closer, tight to his body and never let her go.

Nee-ner, nee-ner, nee-ner. The sirens grew closer and there was more than one.

"Can you walk?"

"Of course I can, I am a Star Marine." He took one step and stumbled, falling to his knees and then rolling into some very prickly bushes. Stars circled above him and they weren't the ones in the night sky.

"Crap. I'm sorry, I should have gotten a better hold on you." Kady's face appeared above his and the stars faded into her eyes. "What if I roll you over to my house?"

"No one is rolling unless it's around in your bed."

There it went again, his cock controlling his mouth. *Get a hold of yourself, bear.*

"You're adorable, but we do not have time for this."

No, no one had ever called him adorable, not even as a cub. Tough, driven, brute, asshole, but never adorable.

"I don't think I can drag you, and I doubt if I covered you

in bushes we'd escape their notice. Hmm." She patted a finger on her lips.

What a beautiful pout she had.

What was wrong with him? Men who wanted to anally probe him were hunting him and his ship down, while the possible lead he had on the spectral soul stealers was growing colder by the minute, and all he could think about was getting her lips around his hardening dick.

If he could get a hard-on, he could get his ass off the ground and walk. "We will walk to your home. Just give me a minute."

"Maybe I can whip up a pair of crutches out of these branches." She lifted the debris of wood he'd created in his fall, rooting around and tossing several branches aside.

"No, lend me your shoulder again. I promise to stay standing if your home isn't too far away."

"Only to the other side of those trees, at the edge of the meadow."

Black glanced in the direction she indicated. The distance wasn't far but felt like the length of twelve fallenball fields. He would have to pull on all his reserves to make it. He was a warrior, an elite Star Marine, and he'd had a lifetime of training, practice, and on the job experience in pushing his body to the Niko.

He sat up, breathed through the pain and got on his feet. He wobbled until Kady slipped under his arm, doing her best to help support him.

"Good job. Ready?"

Again, her touch burned in that amazing way. It must be his injuries. "Ready."

He took one step forward, swayed and leaned heavily onto Kady.

"That's it. One foot in front of the other, and soon we'll be walking out the doo-oo-oor," she sang.

Her voice wavered, and she glanced toward the lights coming toward them.

She was worried. He wanted nothing more in life than to soothe and protect her. The way to do that now was to get out of danger.

He took another step and another. Each felt like he was trying to walk on a ship with two-hundred percent grav plating during a solar storm. Gritting his teeth, they made progress.

Woo-oof. Woo-oof.

Bark, bark, bark, bark, bark, bark, bark.

Aw-ooooooooh.

"What the fuck is that? Do you have three-headed Pardovian aardvarks on this planet?" If so, even calling up his bear, they were screwed.

"Shit buckets. They brought search dogs. We've got to move, mister, alien, dude." Kady tugged at his arm and pulled him into a slow jog.

Each step rattled his bones, several of which were probably broken. Damn. He should have looked through the wreckage of the ship for a med kit.

He shoved the pain aside. "Where is your home, I don't see it."

"Just there, through those trees."

The dog's barking behind them grew louder and closer. The shouts of men's voices could be heard now too.

"I don't think we're going to make it before they hit the clearing."

All their running would be for naught. If they saw him, they would pursue. They needed somewhere to hide. With his next step, Black pivoted and felt something in his ankle snap and crackle. "There, go toward that small hut at the edge of the woods."

"The bathhouse doesn't lock. They'll find you."

"It's our only choice. Go."

Kady nodded and headed for the small hut. "I'll cover you in towels or something."

Ten more meters and they'd be there. Black tripped over his own forsaken feet and they both tumbled to the ground this time. He wrapped his arms around her and took the brunt of the fall to his left shoulder. They rolled several meters and stopped dead when his back hit a tree.

"Are you okay, my Kady?"

"Crfph brrrrrf."

Black lifted his head and stared down at her. "Kady, can you speak? Where are you injured?"

"Can't. Breath."

"Your lungs are damaged?"

"Get. Off."

Black rolled so she was atop him instead of the other way around. "I'll try to be more careful not to crush you the next time you're under me."

Damn fool mouth. Didn't it understand they were in danger.

Kady's deep brown eyes sparkled and she slowly blinked. "Next time?"

"Soon."

"Over there!" A voice sang through the air followed by a cacophony of barking and other shouts.

"Oh no. They're going to see us. Hurry." Kady jumped up and yanked him into the hut through a fabric flap. She tied it shut behind them and then ransacked a small wooden wardrobe next to the door.

"Here, quickly, take off your clothes and get into the hot tub." She threw a large tan towel at him and grabbed another.

Hot tub?

Black stared at the room. "What is this place?"

Dark wood floors surrounded a large white marbled basin with a wooden lid. Opposite was a two-person sized wooden box with a glass door.

If they were on Honaw, this would be the pleasure den of a high-end lady of the night.

"Hurry, they're coming." Kady ripped off her top, tossed her fogging glasses on the bench, and wrapped a towel around herself. She wiggled out of her pants and dropped the clothing into a pile on the floor.

Pleasure den or no, if they were getting undressed, he was all for it. Hopefully she had more of a plan than towels and using her naked body as a distraction.

Although, that was a hell of a good plan. Both his logical brain and the part of him that needed to stake his claim on her agreed.

Black groaned as he took off his shirt and peeled himself out of the carbon-fiber pants. They had protected his legs from the worst of the crash and the subsequent falls. His cock thanked him for that.

Kady flipped the wooden lid off the large basin and he saw it was filled with steaming water. Oh, fuck yeah.

She turned some knobs on the side of the tub and both bubbles and colored lights came on. What a bizarre addition to her pleasure ritual, but one he'd remember. It would hide his wounds and the difference in their skin color should the men in black and their, uh what did she call them? Ah, yes, dogs, come calling.

"Black, get in." Kady was already in the water, but with her towel wrapped around her. He'd get it off her soon enough.

He tossed the towel she'd given him on the little bench next to her glasses and climbed in, one leg at a time. Kady's eyes widened watching him. Her already rosy cheeks went even more red and she turned away.

What a fantastic sexual indicator. A flush of her skin. He could practically see the vasodilation that must be occurring to turn her face and chest such a lovely shade. He'd remember that and make sure to make it happen as often as he could.

These humans were much more interesting than he expected. No wonder the former Star Marine, Niko, had mated one.

Steam from the hot water filled the hut quickly and the warm water felt unbelievable on his sore and broken body. Black waited for the tendrils of pleasure to wash over him.

He'd been more than a little surprised that this human woman would bring him into her bath. Would she be able to resist the water's pleasures? He hoped not.

"Hey, anyone inside?" A voice called from the other side of the hut's fabric door. "We're coming in."

"Yikes, okay. Showtime." Kady looked from the door to Black, visibly gulped and moved across the pool to him.

"Who's there?" her voice lilted, all sweet and innocent. "We're in the hot tub and would rather not be disturbed," she called back.

"Sorry lady, this is a national emergency."

Kady's arms held the towel tight across her ample breasts, but the rest of the material floated around her. His hands developed a mind of their own and wrapped around her waist, pulling her body to his.

She was so damn lush, hips he could sink his big paws into, an ass that went on forever and soft, silky skin. Now if he could get that towel off and reveal what he knew were going to be epic tits.

Having her mostly naked, millimeters away from his raging hard-on, the part of him that cared about saving the universe gave up.

Kady slapped his arm and whispered, "This is not real, so don't go thinking your hands are wandering any further than my waist, mister."

"Whatever you say, *mah wah*." She didn't say he couldn't pull her tight to him, and he did. He might not be feeling the water's pleasure touch, but it was doing wonders for his injuries. The only pain he was feeling was in the hardness of his cock.

"Stay hidden behind me so they don't see your skin."

His injuries were rapidly healing now and his bear

protested to being protected by a female. He'd do the protecting. "I will not hide behind a woman."

"You will, and you'll thank me later, so shut up."

The flap of the doorway opened and Kady wrapped her arms around his neck, whispered, "Universe, help us now," and she threw off the towel and kissed him.

What a fucking kiss it was. She pressed her tongue to his lips, tentatively asking to be let in. She tasted of Anterrian wine and the sweetest dessert. It went straight to his head, and not the one with a brain in it.

"Whoa, whoa, folks. Break it up, and lady, can you put some clothes on, please." A man's voice, like a tree weasel came from the front flap of the tent.

Steam swirled around them, clouding the air in the pleasure den. Kady drew back and blinked.

Black grinned. The kiss had affected her as much as it had him. Good. Because there would be more of it.

While he would try to keep himself concealed from these damn snoops, per her plan, he would defend his woman.

Yes. That was right. She was his.

His mind flashed back to the moment before the crash. His soul ember had lit up like the stars in the sky. He reached for the charm hanging around his neck to thank the Fates for bringing him to his mate.

Wait, where was his amulet? It must be in the wreckage of his shuttle. They'd look for it later, after he got rid of those investigators and fucked the brains out of his beautiful savior.

No, not her brains. She'd laid out a brilliant little plan to fool the fools. He liked her brain.

When they recovered his soul ember, then he could consider the implications to his soul. And hers.

He touched her cheek and then laid a finger over her mouth to keep her in her quietly addled state. "She will do no such thing. This is her home and you are trespassing. She may dress, or undress however she pleases."

Black peeked around Kady enough to see three men, all dressed in black formal-looking clothes, two wearing dark eye-protection, fogging up in the steamy room. The third stood at the fore of the others and was approximately half Black's size. A tree weasel indeed.

"Who's this? Your boyfriend?" The short man, whom Black could crush with his little toe, snickered.

Kady frowned and pushed Black's finger away. She tried to turn, get off his lap, but he didn't let her go far. Instead she looked over her shoulder. "He's, uh, yes, my, uh—"

A flush rose across her cheeks. Was this gorgeous woman who'd had her tongue inside his mouth counting his teeth only mere seconds ago aroused by this disgusting excuse for a human male?

She looked back at him and bit her lip. An unmistakable hurt flashed across her eyes.

She wasn't aroused, she was embarrassed.

His vulnerable siren. Stars in the sky, that was too much for him to handle.

He wanted and needed to make her come a dozen times at least, until she lay sated and forgot all about the rodent of a man behind her.

His hands slipped from her waist to her hips and he pulled her forward, so his cock aligned with her cleft.

Damn, she was wearing an undergarment covering her sex. He gripped the edges of it in his fist, ready to tear it off.

Her mouth popped open, her jaw dropping, and Black remembered their audience, who was waiting for an answer about who he was.

He understood the universal need for men everywhere to prove their worth and knew he could exploit that now. "She uses me for sex. I'm not good enough for her to be seen with in public, but I'll happily take her however I can. Isn't that right, my mistress?"

Her eyes got as wide as the oh of her lips. They were so dark, giant black pools rimmed with amber brown. He could get lost in those eyes. He already was.

The men moved closer, but a communicator crackled, and he heard voices, but couldn't quite distinguish what they were saying. Maybe something about radioactivity? Shit. He damn sure hoped his reactor wasn't leaking.

Tree weasel silenced the communicator, then addressed them again. "Whatever floats your boat, buddy. Did you all see or hear anything strange?"

"What kind of strange?" Kady asked.

Tree weasel came still closer. Much more and Black wouldn't be able to use the steam and Kady as a shield. Against all his instincts he sunk lower in the water.

"You seriously didn't hear that crash?"

This conversation needed to be over, partly to get rid of the investigators and because he wanted to continue the pleasure bath Kady had invited him into. "We've been a distracted if you hadn't noticed, and we'd like to get back to it."

The communicator sounded again, and the voice had a distinct anxious tone saying the word spaceship.

Damn. They had found his ship. He would not be going back to salvage anything now. If the Fates smiled on him, the auto destruct module had survived and would incinerate the vessel before the humans were able to get anything from it.

Black had the distinct feeling the Fates were currently giggling their twisted little asses off.

Tree weasel responded to the communication. "Acknowledged."

The two taller men left the tent, but weasel-boy had to get in the way for one more minute. "Fine. But if you hear or see anything, be sure to let us know."

"Who's us?" Kady had narrowed her eyes but kept her voice all sweetness and light. She was suspicious of this yahoo. That was damn sexy.

"Don't worry about that. We'll check in with you, since the crash, uh, incident site is so close to your hot tub."

Kady's breasts slipped against his chest and Black was more than done with these humans. "Thanks, now get out."

"Listen here, bub."

Little fucker was asking for it. Black would not kowtow to a man who resorted to intimidating women. Weasel reminded him too much of the slave traders that plagued his home world. If he killed the bastard, no more investigator. The others had left, now was his chance.

"I am no bub and if you'd like to take this outside," Black stood to his full two point three-meter height all while holding Kady and her luscious skin tight, her feet dangling in the water in front of him, "I'd be happy to oblige."

The man turned his back and held his arm up acting dismissive. Coward. "Don't get all up in arms. Just keep your eyes and ears open. If you see something, say something."

He popped out of the flap before Black could set Kady down. Too bad, but then they were fantastically alone in the steam and heat and pleasure water.

He'd had enough of duty for today. He could do little else until the swarm of humans retreated. His only duty now was to his mate.

His. Mate.

Black remained standing, wrapped one arm under Kady's ass and lowered his head taking her lips in a hungry kiss.

She kissed him back with such fervor, Black wasn't sure how much longer either of them could wait to join. But then her arms went from around his neck to between them, pushing on his chest.

"Stop right there, asshole."

4

DON'T KISS ME LIKE THAT

This golden-skinned, sexy as sin, alien had just about kissed the daylights, and nightlights, and headlights, and flashlights out of her.

Holy cow balls, the guy had skills. Or maybe it had been too long since she'd been kissed.

Still, she was neither going to bed with a man she's met a half an hour ago, nor having sex with an alien. What if he had, like, two penises, or his penis had teeth, or was covered in fur. Strangely, all the fur she'd seen when they'd been at the crash was gone.

Who knew what alien bodies did? He wasn't of this world. She couldn't assume. But what she did know, just from the feel of him between her legs when they'd kissed… he was effing huge.

She pushed against him, trying to get away from all that deliciousness. He didn't budge. "Put me down."

"I enjoy having you in my arms. I have no intention of letting you go anytime soon."

"Dammit. No means no. You set me down right now or I'll scream bloody murder and bring the men in black back here to dissect you like an insect in a second."

He tilted his head to the side. "Why?"

"Why what?"

"Why do you want me to stop kissing you and put you down. You brought me to your pleasure den, you are turned on by the look of your erect nipples. I will give you many orgasms, and we are safe now. Let us engage in your planet's sexual rituals. Would you prefer to be on the top or the bottom?"

Kady gulped. Many orgasms? Yes, please. Wait, no no no. "Because I don't sleep with men or aliens I've just met."

He searched her face, looking genuinely confused. "Why not?"

His blatant sexual interest in her was overwhelming. Her plan to avoid whatever alphabet agency had worked better than expected. Kissing a fugitive to hide from the bad guys was the oldest ploy in the movies. Obviously, it had convinced this sexy beast too. He'd probably never seen a movie. "Be-be-because."

He nodded. "Ah. Earth customs require me to seduce you first. If you lay on your back I can use my tongue to bring you the first orgasm of our joining."

Kady wriggled out of her giant sex-on-the-brain alien's grasp, his chest hair sliding deliciously over her nipples. She splashed down into the warm water and wrapped her arms around herself, hiding at least part of her exposed boobs. "You and your tongue need to stay away from me."

"Do you not enjoy oral pleasures? Perhaps you do not have that custom in your culture. I promise you will like it.

"I enjoy it just fine. I just don't want it from you." That was a big fat lie. If it weren't for the water, he would be able to see exactly how much her body was begging to let his tongue play with every single part of her. Bad nipples. Bad, bad, nipples.

He took a step closer to her. "Do you not find me attractive? Is my male part not to your liking? It is bigger than the tree weasel's and his lackeys that were just here." Black grabbed his penis and pointed it at her.

She glanced down, and she planned to take only a peek. Her gaze lingered a whole hell of a lot longer than she meant it to. Holy Washington monument, batman. He was huge, like Leaning Tower of Pisa plus Big Ben, plus Ron Jeremy huge. No way that would fit inside anyone's girly bits.

That thing wouldn't even fit in her tiny house.

"I can see you like my cock." He stroked it, and it got incredibly bigger and harder.

"Eep." Kady swished the water pulling herself back, away from the monster cock in her hot tub. In her anxiousness to get away, she forgot her nakedness and stood up, giving Black a full triple D view.

"Double eep." She sank down into the water all the way up to her chin.

"Ah, I see, you prefer to let the pleasure of the water take effect first. But I must warn you, I think the water's powers are deficient. The only touch I have felt has been yours."

"What are you talking about?"

"Perhaps you've over used the waters and their powers

have weakened? I can see how a woman of your beauty is much sought after as a partner. That will have to end. You're mine now."

"Yours? Okay, look." Kady stood again, boobage or not, and pointed her finger at the overbearing alpha-hole. She belonged to no man.

"Oh, I'm looking."

Directly at her naked chest. Crapballs. She sank back down in the water, mortified.

"If my skin flushed as yours does with your arousal I'd be as pink as the Archer nebula. Let me take you, my love. I promise you won't regret it."

"Please get out of the hot tub before I die of heat stroke." Yeah, because that's why she was so hot. Too long in the hot tub. It had absolutely nothing to do with her embarrassment or being so damn turned on that she could faint.

"Only if you are taking me to your bed."

She wiped her brow and the ringing in her ears was back. "I'll do no such—"

Kady swallowed and put out a hand to grab at the side of the tub. Either she was weak in the knees from the advances of this overly sexual alien or she really was getting heat stroke.

"Kady. You've lost your color. What's wrong?"

She wanted to tell him nothing was wrong except that he was being a dick. But instead she fainted.

5

ESCAPE FROM WITCH MOUNTAIN

Black caught Kady in his arms and carried her out of the tub. He laid her on a padded bench and fanned her beautiful face.

Great job he was doing protecting his mate. So far, she'd pulled him from the wreckage of his crashed ship, shielded him from the local law enforcement, called him an asshole, and passed out, either from his advances or the heat.

Not the heat from her desire for him. In fact, she didn't even seem all that attracted to him at all. Except for that kiss, she didn't display any indication that she felt the same pull. His beautiful human didn't seem to know they were bound together for all of time, that she was his fated mate, that she was his.

Forever.

His mate. Strange that the Fates would have him travel hundreds of light years to find her, and in the middle of an intergalactic crisis, none the less. This couldn't have come at a worse time.

He needed to get his head in the game. The instant he saw Kady, his brain had fallen for every impulse his dick demanded. Time to get back in control.

He had ninety-nine problems, but the top two priorities had to be getting to Rogue, New York, and wooing his beautiful new mate.

Normally he had no problem assessing a situation, evaluating the best solution, and putting it into action. It was a large part of why he'd been recruited onto the Elite team in the first place, and how he'd been promoted to leading that team.

Those skills had escaped him when Fate had taken over his life.

The galaxy was depending on him and his team. Since the Fates had decided to interfere, he'd simply have to combine his two goals.

He'd woo Kady while hunting the spectral soldiers. First, they had to get to Rogue, and without his ship he had no knowledge of the terrain, only a vague sense of which direction he needed to go.

Kady would know how to navigate Earth. He knew they weren't far from the destination. He would get her to take him there.

Once he was more fully healed and she was conscious again, he would tell her of his plan. The traveling part, not the wooing part. In his experience, women liked some mystery and intrigue.

Black poked his head out of the bathing tent flap and did some quick reconnoitering. No sign of the tree weasel or his goons. Kady's plan had worked brilliantly. There was activity and voices in the area he'd left his ship behind.

Electra was going to castrate him for allowing this primitive planet to discover their technology, much less get their hands on it.

He'd have to figure out how to deal with that later.

He went back in, pulled on his tattered pants and shirt, then lifted Kady into his arms again. Her skin still seared him in a way that continued to edge up his desire for her. He only hoped they had the evening to themselves. He would begin tantalizing her as soon as she was awake.

Across the small meadow, he spied what must be her abode. It wasn't much bigger than the storage locker on his ship. Why would she live in such a tiny space? Was it an earth custom to have such sparse quarters, but to enjoy the wide-open surrounds? He could live with that. His own home on Honaw, which he hadn't seen in far too long, was at least twenty times the size of hers, but he too had chosen an area to live surrounded by nature.

He crossed the field, limping slightly, but moving fast. The time and waters had more than half healed him. If she was still unconscious when they reached her home, he would become the bear and let the healing powers of the shift finish repairing his wounds.

A small ship with blades that whipped through the air passed overhead and hurried him on. The sooner they could leave the better.

Kady's home was on wheels and was attached to a vehicle. Maybe she was a traveler. Good, because taking her back to Honaw would be a long voyage for her.

The doorway didn't look big enough for him to fit through, much less carrying Kady. He tried and broke some of the wood framing the door with his shoulder.

Another bladed ship approached the field, this one with a search light. It used a standard box search pattern and it wouldn't be long before it reached them.

He'd have to scrap the idea of shifting, or making love to Kady, much to his cock's sorrow. They needed to get out of there and soon.

The back of Kady's vehicle was open and flat. He laid her there as gently as he could and approached the cockpit.

The technology was so ancient it couldn't even be called technology. The only displays were a few dials, and the controls appeared to be a steering wheel, foot pedals and a steel rod lever. That was workable, but he saw no way to start the engine. Maybe it was voice activated?

"Vehicle, start."

Nothing.

"Vehicle, on."

Nope.

"Vehicle, begin ignition sequence."

Okay, so not voice activated.

He should steal one of the bladed ships. He could probably figure out how to fly that easier than Kady's wheeled conveyances.

The search light flashed across the glass shield. They'd changed their search pattern and were moving in to check this part of the field out.

If he didn't figure out how to get the vehicle started and damn soon he'd have to grab Kady and make a run for it into the forest. That had a much lower probability of success.

Black jumped out of the cockpit and moved to the front of the engine housing. He examined the lines of the metal hunk of junk and deduced the best location for a latch. He pulled on it and the casing popped open, thank the Fates.

He used the bear's superior night vision to examine the engine. Combustion. Wow.

No wonder the Earthers had barely made it to manned space missions. What kind of a backwoods planet still used combustion engines. Probably ran on some sort of ancient fuel made of rotting carcasses or something strange too.

He studied the components and, aha, there, wiring that led into the cockpit. The starting mechanism must be wired to the engine from inside.

He ran back and jumped inside. The wires led to the steering column, but the only thing besides the metal was some sort of hanging decoration in the shape of a powerful warrior woman.

Fuck. He ripped open the panels inside the cockpit and found more wiring than he'd bargained for. Combustion meant a firing sequence, and it must be triggered by an electrical current. He chose two wires that had the best chance of connecting and pulled them out.

"Hey. Are you seriously trying to hot wire Herbie? After I saved your ass?" His lovely mate stepped up next to him. She had her glasses on her face, and the towel he was sure he'd left in the pleasure den, wrapped tightly around her. Strange. But she also had a fire in her eyes.

He'd have to remember to push that fire as often as he could. She was gorgeous.

He would do plenty of that as soon as they got to safety, or Rogue. Whichever came first.

"Kady. Thank Fates. How do you start your vehicle? We have to go now."

The bladed ship, with the words Task Force Omega printed boldly on the side, bore down on them and pointed its search light directly on them. A voice came from the sky. "Don't move. This is the TFO. You are being detained for further questioning. Remain where you are."

Kady held her arm aloft and extended only the middle finger toward the ship. Her gesture did not appear to be a sign of surrender. "Screw you, you big bullies."

The metal warrior woman decoration in the vehicle must be Kady's totem.

"Push down on that pedal, right there." She indicated the pedal to his far left and he depressed it.

Nothing happened. She reached across him, twisted the totem and the engine sputtered to life.

Noted. Pedal, then totem twist. "Get in."

Kady bolted across the front of the vehicle.

"Halt, or we'll shoot." The TFO didn't wait and fired a weapon that bounced off the corner of the engine housing with a loud clang.

Kady ducked down and crawled on her hands and knees to the side door. No way was Black allowing these Earthers to use weapons against his mate. He roared, letting his bear rise to the surface.

His canines and incisors elongated, and his claws burst forth, weapons he would use on anyone who harmed Kady.

"Whoa. That explains the fur." Kady peered at him from a crouched position on the side of the open door. She tried to stand, but another volley of the weapon rained down on them, puncturing the vehicle's metal.

"Shit, Herbie."

Shouts came from behind them and they both turned to see a whole squad of the TFO men moving toward them at a rapid clip.

They had maybe three minutes before they were swarmed. He could not allow them to capture him or touch Kady.

The second bladed ship flew in over the trees and hovered just above them, its lights illuminating the cockpit.

"Kady, we have to move."

"I have a plan. Can you distract them? Maybe with more of that animal thing you got going on?"

"I must protect you."

"Protect me later, first, cover me." Kady bolted, running for the tiny home. Fucking hell.

Black shifted fully, his bear pouring forth from his soul faster than it had ever come on. He rolled from the Herbie and stood up to his full bear height and roared so loud it echoed off the mountains.

That drew the TFO's fire. Shots of metal bit into his shoulder and still he snarled. Fear poured from the men on the ground and he would use that to drive them away.

He charged toward the closest men, taking fire, but pushing them to retreat. The first few rounds went clean through him and his wounds healed easily. Another squad emerged and flanked him shooting at his back.

He turned on the closest of the men and lashed out, tearing them down like children's toys. More men fired and this time the projectiles lodged in his body. The bear's healing powers pushed some of the metal bits out, but there were more hitting him than his body could deal with.

He'd have to either turn and run, leading them away, or charge and hope he could last against the barrage for as long as it took for Kady to escape.

Black roared again, and his muscles bunched in preparation to take out the line of men firing at him.

Before he could move, Kady appeared on the porch of her home, a small black box and wiring leading into the house under her arm.

A weapon?

"Come on universe. Gimme some cloud cover," she said.

The billows of smoke from the fires started by his crash and a quickly building bank of clouds closed in over the field. The bladed ships were engulfed and moved off.

Fates above. Had Kady done that?

She squatted down, pointed one end of the box toward the sky and flipped open a cover to reveal a white light.

A squadron of fighter ships appeared in the sky, seeming to appear right as the clouds did, surprising both Black and the TFO men. The men raised their weapons and fired.

Kady aimed a small handheld control at the interior of her home and the sound of the ships whooshed through the sky. Laser fire sounded, pew pew pew, and they could all hear the communications of the star fighters.

"Red leader one..."

"He's on my tail, I can't shake him."

"It's a trap!"

Black looked up at the battle raging in the sky, and then over at Kady.

"Don't just stand there, you big bear, help me unhitch the trailer."

Black used all his energy to run to her side and fell beside her. The last hits of the weapons had weakened him.

"Oh no. Black. You can't die now." She touched his muzzle imbuing him with her own spirit. The flow of her soul to his buzzed like a shot of alcohol spreading warmth through him. It was enough to get him back on his feet.

The Fates had given him a powerful mate. He only hoped he was good enough for her.

Kady pushed on the metal bar connecting the Herbie and the little house, turning the crank on a hand wheel at the same time. "These schmoes are only going to fall for those X-wing fighters for about two more seconds. Come on, universe. Gimme a little help."

The metal ball and socket holding the whole thing together fell apart right before his eyes. That was the second time Kady had used those words and made her will happen.

Hot damn. How had he not noticed it before? His mate was a witch. A much more powerful one than any he'd seen on his home world.

"Go, Black, go." She pushed him toward the Herbie.

"God. You're not going to fit. Can you turn back into a man?"

Black pushed the bear back inside, again shifting faster than normal. That had to be from her powers as well.

"Yes," he said.

"Okay then. Get in the truck. The Death Star is about to explode."

Sweet Fates, what did that mean? Just how powerful was his witch?

They both jumped into the vehicle. Kady started it up and pushed on the accelerator. They screeched across the field and down a hidden dirt road. As they flew into the cover of the trees, behind them a loud explosion boomed and then the sounds of cheering reverberated through the air.

"Did the TFO destroy your weapon?"

"No, the rebels just defeated the Empire."

Black looked at her wondering what Empire she could possibly mean. Had the Taarians been trying to take over this portion of the galaxy and he'd been so tied up in the hunt for the spectral soldiers he hadn't known?

There was so much more to Kady than he expected. Her powers could help in the battle against the spectrals. The sooner they could hook up with his team the better.

"Don't worry," Kady said, "The Empire will strike back."

6

IN THE GARDEN OF GNOMES

Herbie flew down the mountain, so fast she thought he might fall apart. Kady had never seen him go above fifty, but they were doing ninety miles an hour trying to get away from the TFO.

She took a turn like a Formula One driver, which she was not. But the steering wheel easily gliding through her hands and Herbie floated around the bends in the road and over the rocks and dirt.

Maybe her alien bear man was using a special power to help them escape. Good, because they could use all the help in the universe. If the TFO was after them, they were totally screwed.

She'd read the conspiracy theories, from Area 51 to the ancient aliens of Nazca. But that's all they have ever been, fun to think about, but not reality. But then again, she thought the same about aliens up until a few hours ago.

Kady glanced over at Black. He had transformed back into a man, a man who was bleeding all over the place.

"We have to get you to a hospital. No, wait scratch that. We need to get somewhere with Internet, so I can watch a YouTube video or something to figure out how do first aid on bullet wounds."

There was a video for everything on YouTube. At the very least there would be an episode of Grey's Anatomy.

She glanced down at the towel, that had somehow stayed on her body through all that, and wished for a Wal-Mart.

"No. Keep going. Put as much terrain between them and us as you can. I'll be fine. When we find a safe place, you can use your powers to heal where my bear has not."

They hit Devils Gulch Road and evening traffic buzzed by. Okay, two cars drove by but an old red pickup going ninety would stick out. They would be less conspicuous if she went the speed limit. They'd need to find a place to hide quick.

Black sunk deeper into the bench seat, looking less golden and more pale by the second. "Why did you not tell me you were a witch?"

Loosing blood or no, there was no reason to get assholey. "Hey. Don't be calling me names. I just saved your ass. Again."

Three big dark SUVs with tinted windows passed them going toward her home and the crash site. The longer they stayed out in the open, the more chance someone was going to spot them and capture them and probe them.

Kady did not want to be probed. Unless it was by Black's tongue. What, wait, whoa. No. That must be the adrenaline talking. Yeah, yeah, the complete and total attraction to a bear-shifting, alpha male, alien was because of a hormone.

"Is witch a derogatory term in your culture? What do women who can manipulate the world around them with their will call themselves? Your powers are far beyond anything the I have seen on my home world."

"What powers? The power of an LCD projector and high-speed internet?" The closer to town they got, the more rubber-necking tourists they encountered. They passed at least five cars pulled over to the side of the road. Usually people stopped to stare and take pictures of the wildlife that wandered around the town down from the sanctuary of Rocky Mountain National Park. These gawkers were all focused on the billows of smoke and line of emergency vehicles speeding up the mountain.

Kady glanced over at Black and found him frowning at her. Not like he was mad, but like he couldn't figure her out. That was not a first.

"Stop staring at me like that and help me find a place we can hide both us and Herbie."

He did not stop staring. "I know of a place we will be safe, but it is not nearby."

"I'll take anything at the moment. Unless you mean your home planet. I don't think we have enough gas for that." Although, for being an ancient truck, Herbie got excellent gas mileage.

Black pointed toward the south. "No. Do you know how to get to New York?"

"Oh, my god. Are you taking me to your mother ship there?" She'd always wanted to go to New York.

"I don't know any area by that designation, and my mother does not have a ship, she has, had a farm. We need to get to a place called Rogue, New York. There are more of your kind there and my team is waiting for me."

Her kind? Like plump nerdy girls who didn't much like people and preferred to live in sci-fi and fantasy worlds on TV and in books? The only place she'd ever been that had people like her was ComicCon.

"We need someplace closer than New York. You're wounded, and Herbie isn't exactly inconspicuous." Maybe they could get lost in the traffic in Denver. First, they had to get there.

"We should head in that direction. Do you have any friends we could take refuge with?"

Friends were not her strong suit. She'd been better off on her own, up in the woods, in her tiny house.

That was probably now swarming with TFO agents who were examining every bit of her pathetic life.

"Not really." Kady glanced over at Black, expecting to see that disdain everyone who was cooler than she was got when she had to admit her shortcomings.

He looked decidedly ungolden. His injuries were taking a toll on him. "Can you call your team and have them come get you?"

He shook his head. "My communicator is likely still in the remains of my ship."

Her cell phone was back in the remains of her tiny house. Damn. "Won't they come to rescue you?"

"No. The mission they are on is more important than one man. Which is why we must get to New York."

Once they got past the lake, she got on US 34 to head down the mountain. But that road was only two lanes, and there were not a lot of options to get off if the TFO showed up.

Which they did, right then and there.

One of the big dark SUVs they'd seen earlier drove up behind them and rammed her bumper. "Holy crap. They're going to kill us."

There were only trees, a cliff, and the steep slope of a mountain on either side of the road. If they tried to run her off, she and Black would either end up Thelma and Louis-ing off the cliff or crashing through the trees. Black had already done that once today.

"Go, Kady, go. I will try to find a way to defend us." Black opened the glove box and found Herbie's service records, a box of breath mints, an aux cord, and nothing else.

He crumpled the papers and tossed them out the window. One stuck to the SUVs windshield, but their wipers took care of that instantly.

The TFO bad guys gunned it and pulled up next to her, then plowed into the side of Herbie, making her swerve onto the shoulder.

"I suggest you call upon the Universe to help us."

"I don't think the law of attraction works like that."

"Do it, Kady. Say your spell."

The SUV rammed them again.

What the hell. "Dear sweet Universe, help us not die and get away from the bad guys."

They took the next turn, screeching around the corner and straight into a thick bank of fog. Kady couldn't see a thing, but she knew the cliff edge was to their left and the forest was to the right.

She'd rather end up smashed into a tree than smashed into the canyon floor a trillion feet below them.

She jerked the steering wheel to the right and Herbie flew into the ditch, into the trees and down a small incline. Kady did the best she could to steer. Tree branches slapped the windows and they bumped over the rocks and other terrain. The ground below them dipped and she lost all control of the truck floating through the air. Please don't let them have gone over the cliff.

One minute they were bouncing off trees, and the next they were at a complete stand still.

Kady breathed in and out. It was all she could muster for a moment. How had they stopped? They hadn't crashed. They'd simply stopped moving forward. Maybe they had plowed into a tree and were dead now.

"Kady, are you okay? Are you injured." Black was breathing as fast as she was, but he seemed unharmed too.

"I'm fine, I think. Unless we died in a fiery crash and don't know it yet."

Black pointed out the window. The fog bank lifted, leaving as suddenly as it had rolled in. "I think not, unless your afterlife is a green field surrounded by large metal boxes."

In front of them, a small serene meadow sat dotted with tiny houses made from shipping containers. Behind them was a forest of thick trees, none of which seemed disturbed by their violent entry.

How? What?

A small person, like really short and stocky with a long white beard, popped out the front door of one of the houses.

If Kady were less PC, she'd have said he was a garden gnome minus his hat.

She couldn't hear him, but he was waving his arms and yelling across the field at them. Then a second small person, a woman wearing a yellow dress and an apron came out and starting yelling at the man.

"Do you know these gnomes?" Black asked.

She smacked him on the arm. "Don't call them that. They're little people."

"The little people are approaching. We should ask them for shelter." He opened the door and got out of Herbie.

She followed him out, but only to stop him. "Wait, they don't look very friendly."

"We will be able to evade the TFO with them. Come, *mah wah.*" Black took her hand and led her across the field.

"You," the man pointed at Kady, "what do you think you're doing coming in on a cloud and invading our garden?"

The woman tsked. "Now, dear. Don't make the pretty witch and her bear mad. I'm sure if they needed to break through our wards there is a good reason."

The little woman said some foreign sounding words, waved her hand in the air, and a quick buzz, like a bee flying by shot over their heads. "There, that fixes that."

Black put his body between the little people and Kady. Like he had when the TFO had been firing at her. Both times this strange tingling happened below her breastbone.

"We require your assistance," Black said.

Great, way to get on the angry little man's good side. She might not have all that many social skills, but at least she could apologize and start them off on a better foot.

"Sorry, we couldn't see where we were going in all that fog. We didn't mean to invade or break your, uh, wards." Whatever those were. Kady glanced at Black's wounds, her own towel dress and then to the woman, hoping for some empathy. "But we were run off the road and we could really use your help."

"Oh, yes. Come, come, we'll put you in the house Sigar just completed." She indicated they should follow her and walked toward one of the containers. "It's on order for another witch so the interior should be the right size for the two of you."

Maybe Kady had bonked her head in the crash down the mountain because these people were saying some things she couldn't wrap her mind around. Another witch?

The man stomped his foot. "Margreth, you always do this. We are not doing anything for these people. They broke into our garden, trouble is following them, and I have to ship that house tomorrow."

Margreth tsked him again and then bopped him on the nose. "Shush yourself, Sigar. Everything will be fine. The bear needs our help and you can still ship your beautiful house tomorrow."

Sigar seemed to like the compliment and to get his nose bopped because he rolled his eyes and pretended to still be mad, but there was an unmistakable grin on his face.

"Will your broom be okay in the grass?" Margreth indicated to Herbie and then led them to one of the containers.

"My truck? Sure. The grass is fine."

The shipping container turned into a house had been painted a beautiful light blue on top with grass and trees to blend in with the scenery below, a whole bay of windows had been added, and it even had a covered porch. It was bigger, and much nicer than Kady's tiny house. A stylized graphic of a garden gnome had been stamped on the door. Under it were the words Gnome Sweet Home, Inc.

"Oh. You're Sigar Gunderson of Gnome Sweet Home? I looked at buying one of your tiny houses earlier this year."

Sigar harrumphed. "Why didn't you then?"

"Well, to be honest, you were a bit out of my price range." By about fifty grand.

"You could have asked for the magical people discount, dear." Margreth waved her hands in front of entryway and the door popped open.

Cool, motion sensors. "Uh, I didn't know that was a thing. I'm not really into magic."

The Gundersons and Black stared at her.

"What? Do I have something on my face? Are there branches in my hair?" She wiped at her face and patted her head. Had her towel slipped?

She yanked on the terry cloth and made sure it was still in place.

Margreth and Black exchanged a look. The kind that people who know something you don't, give each other. Black shook his head.

"She doesn't know?" Margreth asked.

"Know what?" This was why she didn't like to be around people. Even with an alien and two people who resembled garden gnomes she still felt like an outsider.

"I don't think she does," Black replied.

"I'm right here. What don't I know?"

Sigar walked inside the house and they all followed him. No one said a word.

Kady could feel the heat rising up her neck and chest. They were all staring at her and she wanted to find a hole to climb into.

Sigar crossed his arms. "But she broke our wards and created that cloud you floated in on. She's powerful. How can she not know?"

Kady swallowed, twice. "Please tell me what you think I don't know.

Margreth smiled in the way a grandmother who is about to give out presents did. "My dear, a powerful magic lives inside of you. You used it to enter our garden which is protected so non-magical folk can't find it. You're traveling with a bear in man form, a familiar, and a broom."

None of this made any sense. Aliens she could buy into. But magic, like the kind out of Hogwarts? No way. That was true fantasy, kind of like love and happy ever afters for geeky chubby girls who wore glasses and grew up in foster care.

Some people believed in both. Kady wasn't one of them.

She shook her head.

Margreth, Sigar, and Black all nodded theirs.

She looked at Black, searching his face. He wasn't laughing at her, none of them were. In fact, his gaze had both heat and honesty there.

He reached out taking her shoulders and pulled her into his arms. "Kady," he brushed his lips across hers and cupped her cheek in his hand." My sweet *mah wah*, you are a powerful magic-wielding witch."

7

THUNDER, LIGHTNING, AND SNOW

Black's luscious mate was not taking the news that she was more than an ordinary human very well. He wasn't sure what he expected her reaction to be, but the stark stillness that enveloped her body was not it.

"We'll go make some food and drink, and let you two be, then shall we?" Margreth grabbed her husband and dragged him out the door.

Good. He needed time to tend to his mate and then his own wounds. Once he was sure she was all right, he would shift and heal the remaining injuries.

By the look on Kady's face, that wouldn't be for a while. She needed time and comfort. One he could give, the other they had precious little of.

He lifted her into his arms and headed for the back of the strange little abode. There had to be a bed where she could rest.

"Whoa. You can't pick me up and carry me around. I'm too heavy, you'll drop me on my ass."

Ah, there was his Kady.

"I assure you, *mah wah*, you are the perfect size and I will never drop you." Her ass was his to savor and protect.

"Where do you think you're taking me, and why do you keep calling me that?"

"I am taking you to bed."

She poked him in the chest. That fire inside her sparking to life again. "No, you are not. Stop right there, alien, bear-man, whatever. Put me down."

He should heed her wishes, but he didn't. If he had to spark her ire to continue to bring her back from shock, he'd do everything he could to piss her off.

The flush that made her so tempting spread across her skin. He was beginning to recognize the different emotions based on the shades of her skin. The anger was pretty, but he wanted to again see the blush of sexual excitement.

He kicked open the door to the bedroom and laid her on the bed. How he wanted to crawl in with her, pleasure her, make her forget ninety-nine percent of this day had ever happened. All except for the part when they'd kissed.

She'd been through more than enough for today. She needed food, drink, and a good sleep. He would take care of her, protect her, defend her, comfort her, and when she was ready, pleasure her, claim her, mate her.

He reached for his ember and felt its absence keenly.

"Hey, where are you going?"

"You've have been a fierce warrior today, pulling me from the wreckage of my ship, hiding me from the TFO tree weasel in your pleasure den, making them think battle ships were attacking so we could escape, and finding a refuge. It is my turn to take care of you. Rest, while I make food."

Of course, she didn't. She flipped her legs over the side of the bed and moved to get up. He growled and tackled her, pushing her back into the bed and under him. As it should be. His soul cried out to claim her now, make her his forever.

He pinned her arms above her head and pressed his hips to hers, letting her feel how hard and ready his body was and had been all evening for her.

"Don't move from this bed, *mah wah*. I will never hurt you, but you are mine to take care of, especially when you won't take care of yourself."

Her mouth popped open into a surprised oh, and he couldn't help but lick her round little lips. "You have had enough for today. Rest, or I will make you rest."

She pushed against him, but without using her magic, couldn't move him even a little. He watched her struggle, waited for her to wear herself out.

"I'll...I'll use a magic spell on you."

Fates, she was pretty when she was mad. "You don't know any."

She wrinkled up her nose wiggled it and her lips back and forth. A tiny storm cloud formed over their heads.

Uh-oh, maybe her magic instincts were about to revolt. He hoped she planned to rain on his head and not strike him with lightening.

Three giant fluffy snowflakes drifted out of the cloud, one sticking in his hair, one landed on the pillow, and another on her eyelashes.

The fire in her eyes banked and she stopped fighting

against him. Her lack of powers defeated her. He would do his best to help remedy that as soon as they were safe in New York.

"Good girl."

She stuck her tongue out at him.

He was sure it was meant as a slight, but all he wanted to do was tangle his own with hers. "Sometime soon I'll ask you to do that again. But for now, rest while I make us some food."

"I'm not hungry."

"But you are stubborn. If I get up will you stay?"

She rolled her eyes at him. "Fine."

Black released her arms and she didn't move. He couldn't resist one quick kiss. He stole the kiss from her, pressing his tongue inside to say hello to hers and make promises for more later, then got up before he couldn't resist and stayed.

He stood over her for a moment, ready to push her down, should she get up again, but she turned on her side and cuddled into the pillow.

"I'll be right back."

He hurried to the door to check with the gnomes about food and if they had a communications device. When he opened the door, he found tray with food, glass jars of water, a small container, and a note.

We've reinforced the wards, so you two will be safe to rest until morning. We've coaxed the big broom into another container for the night. The small jar has a little healing salve for your wounds.

Sleep well,

The Gundersons

Black took the food and salve to the bedroom where he found Kady asleep. Make that talking in her sleep.

"George Lucas...you can't do that to Captain Picard."

Hmm. Sounded like Kady had many other men in her life. He would have to work hard to make her forget all of them. Starting now.

He should eat, shift, and let his bear finish healing his wounds, but he was too damn tired, and curling up with his mate was too tempting. He stripped off his clothes and crawled into the bed gently pulling Kady into his arms.

"Help me, Obi Bear Kenobi, you're my only hope."

He drifted off listening to her have a conversation with a droid named R2-D2 who needed a good reprogramming for all its shenanigans.

His dreams were filled with spectral soldiers, stealing the souls of everyone around him. He offered his own soul in trade for leaving Kady's.

"Black? Black, are you awake?" Kady was wrapped tight in his arms and whispered against his chest.

"What is it, *mah wah*?" He ran his hands over her arms and back, needing to reassure himself she was safe and secure.

She didn't pull away but grasped his arm. "You're bleeding again."

Sure enough, one of the wounds from the TFO weapons seeped blood down his arm. "It's okay, my body is trying to heal."

She was quieter in the dark of the night, like she's been awake thinking for a long time. "We need to get you some medical care."

Black didn't want her to move, even for a second. It might break the spell they were in, the one where he got to hold her and touch her and hopefully she wanted to be held and touched.

She hadn't tried to get away from him when she awoke. She'd spooned into him and seemed comfortable in his arms. "No, I'll be fine once I shift. My bear can heal me faster than anything else, unless you want to try your magic."

She looked up into his eyes, and was so close, so soft, he needed to kiss her.

She placed her fingers on his chest, playing with the skin where his soul ember should be hanging. Did she sense its importance to their relationship too?

He could see her mind working, she was deciding on something. "You should do that, change into the bear."

She was avoiding saying what was truly on her mind. This might be the only time they have in the foreseeable future. It was the perfect opportunity to draw her out, to woo her. The battles ahead were not exactly the best time to start a relationship.

"I'd rather lie here with you in my arms, *mah wah*. That's harder to do with paws and claws."

She didn't look up, avoiding his eyes. "What does that word mean, the one you keep calling me?"

"*Mah wah*? There isn't a good equivalent in your language or the translator would have chosen it. It's something like sweetheart, and lover, and soul mate all rolled into one."

She frowned and tried to pull away from him. "Why would you call me that? I mean, I like you, more than seems normal, but you're like a thousand percent hotter than me. I'm not the kind of girl someone like you, calls something like that."

The bear inside roared at the outrage of her words. It rose to the surface, close to the shift, pouring its energy through him, healing the last of his wounds, ready to defend his mate.

His Kady had been hurt, more than once, if he had to guess. He wanted nothing more than to eat the faces off anyone who had ever made her doubt herself in this way.

So sweet, so vulnerable. He contained the bear and breathed her in. "I'm sorry you feel that way. Let me show you how wrong you are."

He lifted her chin and brushed his lips across hers, asking for more. At first, she stiffened, but when he skimmed his fingers along her neck, and gently took her bottom lip between his teeth, her eyes fluttered shut and she responded with a soft sigh.

She wanted to be touched, to be pleasured, she needed it. He would be the one to give her everything she needed.

He rolled so she was under him and he could caress and touch her whole body. He wasn't wearing anything, but she was in the towel. "Use your magic, pretty witch, make your clothes disappear so I can touch every bit of your luscious body."

"I don't know how."

He kissed the soft skin behind her ear, licking and

learning how to turn her on. "You do, use your spell, ask the Universe for help."

"Oh, mmm, do that again." She clasped her hands into his hair and pulled his mouth back down.

He obliged, sucking and nibbling from her ear down to her chest. "I can lick you in many more places if you were naked."

"I feel strange asking the Universe to help me get some sexy times. Let's just take my towel off."

The top fold of Kady's towel wriggled and Black hoped her powers were manifesting. Instead a small creature stuck its head out.

He stilled, instantly forming a plan to rid them of the creature and not break the sexual tension they were building. "Do not be alarmed. There is a spiky rodent sticking out of your clothing. Stay as still as you can and I will dispose of it."

She blinked, and alertness came into her eyes. "Don't you touch Percy."

Percy?

She wiggled her nose like she'd done before and her towel and the creature disappeared and manifested on the table next to the bed.

"Ha ha. I did it." She giggled, and a smile lit up her face.

"Yes, you did." And she should be rewarded for her skill. Black lowered his head and sucked her now exposed nipple into his mouth. Fates, she was so sweet.

"Oh, my god. Ooh, Black." Kady's hands pushed back into his hair, holding him to her breast.

He'd work to make sure her hands were occupied all night. He licked and sucked and nibbled making her moan.

Her other breast needed attention too. He cupped it, loving the way it filled his hand. Her nipple pressed hard against his palm.

"More, Black. Please."

"Your undergarment, Kady, I'll give you more when you make it disappear too."

She closed her eyes, wiggled her nose, and her undergarment joined her towel on the table.

"Fates above, you are fucking gorgeous."

The flush of her skin, he'd waited too long to see, crept across her chest, neck, and skin. With a wrinkle of her nose, there was nothing between him and Kady anymore.

Except the sheet she pulled across her legs and belly. "You don't need to see those jiggly bits."

Black growled low in his throat. "Oh, yes. I do."

He ripped the sheet from her body and threw all the bed coverings onto the floor. Now he had Kady in all her naked glory, her body ready to explore.

"Eep." She crossed her legs and thrust her arms over her sex.

"Don't try to hide from me, *mah wah*. Don't deny me your beauty." He grabbed her hands and pushed them over her head. She bit her lip and turned her face away from him.

Once he claimed her and showed her over and over again how desirable she was, she would never have to be ashamed of her body...ever.

He pushed his thigh between hers, opening her. The scent of her sex wafted over his senses, pushing his bear toward the feral need to take her. Soon she would be his, but not yet.

"Kady, look at me."

She closed her eyes.

"Let me see the fire and lust inside of your soul. I need it, I need you."

Her eyes flew open, and she looked at him surprised. That was all the advantage he needed. He slid his hand between her legs and caressed her inner thigh, coaxing her to open for him.

"Don't look away. Let me see the desire, the passion building in you."

Kady swallowed and licked her lips. Slowly, she spread her legs, giving him access to her plump pussy.

8

BABY, YOU'RE A FIREWORK

Sex had never been like this, and they hadn't even gotten to the main event yet.

For Kady, sex had been a fumbling, under the covers, lights out, ten-minute deal with guys she told herself cared, but who she knew didn't really.

Not with Black, he wanted her. His need was palpable, and yet so far, it had been all about her. God, he was being so sweet and gentle. Nothing like any other guy she'd ever been with.

He wasn't like any other guy. He was sexy, and rugged, and the exact opposite of the Nikoi-zoom-dweebs she'd dated before.

Not that they were dating.

"Open yourself to me." Black stroked over Kady's skin, never taking anything until she gave it.

Man, did she want it. Every touch sent fire burning through her. There was something more than just foreplay going on here. A deep need glowed in the base of her spine.

He held her hands securely above her head, so she couldn't move. He was in control, guiding everything that happened, and she found a freedom in that. A way she could relax and let anxiety fall away.

She spread her legs, letting go of the fears that her body wasn't good enough. If Black wanted it, her, she would give herself to him, and enjoy it while it lasted.

"That's it." Finally, he dipped into her folds. She knew she was already wet, ready for him. "Mmm, your body is so responsive, so beautiful."

She still had a hard time believing that, but she wanted to, and that was enough for now. "Please, Black. I want you inside of me."

"Like this?" He pushed two fingers in, filling her, stroking.

"Ohh, yes." Her back arched of its own accord, trying to get more of him. She closed her eyes, trying her best to only feel.

"Look at me, Kady. Let me see how good I make you feel." Black slid his thumb over her clit, back and forth, spiking the pleasure pulsing through her.

She dragged her eyes back open and found his. They were dark and sparkled with lust. She could so easily fall in love with him.

"Tell me what you like, what you want."

"This." She lifted her head and kissed him. She licked his bottom lip and sucked it into her mouth. He tasted like Thanksgiving and Christmas, the deep woods on a crisp winter day, a crackling fire and a hot cup of spiced wine. He tasted of home.

"Fates above, your kisses are so sweet. I don't know how you do that, but I want so much more." Black kissed her harder, his tongue dancing in and out of her mouth, tangling with hers.

His fingers matched the dance, crooking inside of her, finding just the right spot to make her cry out. "Black. Black. Don't stop."

"Yes, my sweet Kady, that's it."

They'd barely begun and Kady had never gotten this turned on this fast. It was like Black knew exactly what her body needed, when it needed it, to drive her closer to coming.

"Look at me when you come. Let me see your soul on fire for me."

She stared into his eyes, that seemed to glow. Her breathing was coming in fast gulps of air, her skin prickled with awareness of every molecule in the room, they all caressed her, joining with Black to push her to the brink of exploding.

Golden wisps floated through the air, wafting from her skin to his, surrounding them both.

"Kady, my Kady, come for me, my love. Come for me."

Kady cried out, calling Black's name, and the room exploded into a million sparkles, like the light of the sunrise across an endless ocean. Her body and mind floated in the pleasure, held to Earth only by the anchor of Black holding her there, sharing in the glow.

Black released her arms and pulled her close to him, stroking her back, and her hair. He was warm and safe, and all the things she needed.

When she could breathe again, she could speak again. "What was that?"

He kissed her on the top of the head. "You, love, sharing your soul with me."

"Does that always happen during alien sexy times?"

Black chuckled. "No, I've only heard that it can happen between fated mates."

Fated mates? Like they were mates now? That wasn't how love worked. She only knew she was drawn to him, no, more than that. She wanted to be near him, with him.

"Black, what is this thing between us? I have all these feelings for you, but I hardly know you."

So, why was she in bed with him now? It didn't feel like a mistake, but her mind said it must be.

He was quiet for a minute. "It's the Fates. They have put us together. I knew you were my mate the second I saw you. My soul ember, the bit of my soul pulled from me and placed into an amulet, began to glow before I even hit the ground. It knew you were close and that you were mine."

Kady sat up, grabbed the sheet from the floor and wrapped it around herself, giving her mind a minute to wrap around this idea. "Fate? Like we were pre-destined to be together?

She wasn't sure she liked the sound of that, being a fan of free will and all.

Black watched her, a wariness, a worry crossing his face. "You were chosen for me, and I for you, but ultimately we still have a choice. If we decide we don't want to be together, it will be difficult." He took her hand and stroked the soft skin of her palm. "There will be an emptiness in our souls that can never be filled, but I have seen others do it, go on to live without mates."

He was giving her an out, and the pain that caused him sparked across their connection. It hurt. An ache built at the base of her throat. "We don't have to be, like, married tomorrow or something?"

"No, *mah wah*. If we were on Honaw I would court you, seduce your mind first and then your body. Our run in with the TFO and my mission has turned things around, and I'm sorry for that."

"Court me?" She wrinkled up her nose. Sounded so old-fashioned. But maybe she could use a little of that in her life.

"You are the only one for me, forever, I know that deep in my heart, down to my soul, even without the ember." He swallowed and tipped his head. "If you don't want to be with me, you don't have to. Because as hard as it would be to be separated, it would be even worse to feel forced to be together."

A vulnerability she never expected, poured off him. This, from a giant of a man, who could turn into an even bigger bear, and who had just given her a soul scorching orgasm.

She wanted to soothe him, but was it even possible?

"Can we even be together. You're an alien bear shifter and I'm—" She couldn't say it. She couldn't believe it.

"A beautiful, sensuous human witch. There is no physical or biological reason a bear and a witch can't be together."

She bit at her lip, wanting to accept his words, but finding it hard. "That whole witch thing is way weird."

He played his fingers across her skin, touching such benign places on her body, like the inside of her wrist, the crook of her elbow. Each caress built the fire inside for him again.

"It doesn't have to be. There are others like you."

Ha. Yeah, right. "I doubt that. Other people aren't like me. Other people don't even like me."

He lifted her chin with his knuckled and stroked her cheek. "I like you."

She found anything else in the room to look at, but him. Because if she did, he'd see the stupid sloppy grin his words had put on her face. "You're just trying to get in my pants."

"I believe I was in your pants about ten minutes ago."

"Okay, that's true." She took a deep breath. Why not accept the good the Universe or the Fates or whoever had brought her? The last few hours had been the craziest, and best in her life. She'd be a fool to not grab on and never let go. "Where do we go from here?"

Black smiled and pushed her back on the bed. He kissed her and kissed her and kissed her until she could hardly think. He stripped the blankets from the bed again and settled himself between her legs.

"First, I'm going to make you come another six times, at least."

Six? "Umm, how about we split the difference. I get three and you get three."

She could feel his cock pressing against her, and it liked her idea better. She wiggled her hips against him and laughed when his eyes rolled back in his head and he growled.

"That is no way for a bear to treat his mate. You'll get six and like it."

She had no doubt about that. "Don't make me use my magic on you. I can make it snow, I'll have you know."

He started kissing his way down her body, stopping at each breast, making her lose her mind. Right before he got to her upper thighs, he stopped. "You can do a lot more than that, *mah wah*. Tomorrow, I'll show you. Tonight, I'll show you my powers."

He spread her legs and kissed her upper thigh, then the softest part of her inner thigh. Soon he was doing a whole lot more than kissing her thighs.

He licked and suckled her clit, sending pure carnality coursing through her. It didn't take long before the colors and sparkles carried her away.

He didn't let up until she cried mercy. Five orgasms later. She hadn't even thought that was possible. He was the one with magic powers.

"Black, please. No more. It's your turn, please, let it be your turn."

He crawled up her body and kissed her. She tasted herself on his tongue and lips. She was beyond sated, but he hadn't even come yet.

"You owe me one more orgasm."

She held his face in her hands. "I don't think I can."

"What if I do this?" He tilted his hips forward so the head of his cock pushed in exactly the right spot.

"Oh, god. Maybe."

"And this?" He pressed forward, slowly entering her, stretching her. If her body wasn't already relaxed from the orgasmpalooza, she doubted he'd fit. He tilted his hips, pushing into her, never taking his eyes off her, filling her, deliciously.

She slanted her body, meeting his, completing their joining. Their bodies together, as one, felt right, complete.

Black withdrew and thrust again, then again. She matched the cadence he set, their bodies dancing in perfect harmony. With every movement, their pleasure increased, and a soft glow emanated from them.

Black made love to her, coaxing the pleasure from her body. Golden swirls raised from their skin, or from a deeper place inside, lighting up the room. With each touch of Black's body to hers, the lights intensified.

This time, Kady had no problem believing in what she was seeing. Before the light had come only from her, but now Black's soul was aflame and intermingled with her own.

Her own light reached for his, swirling together all around them like smoke and embers from a fire, but much more beautiful.

She wrapped her legs around the back of his thighs, holding him closer, never wanting to let him go. The light mixed with their emotions, with their desires, multiplying it.

Black buried his face in the crook of her neck, pressing his lips to her pulse point. "Kady, I've never felt anything like this before, fuck, you're amazing."

He reached between them and found her clit, so sensitive. With each thrust of his cock inside of her, he stroked his fingers over her, pushing her toward pure bliss.

"Come for me one more time, *mah wah,* I need to feel your hot pussy come on my cock. Tell me you're close, because I'm not going to last much longer."

"Come with me, Black. Make me yours."

Black growled deep from within, and bit at the skin of her shoulder. He lost the rhythm and drove into her wildly, stretching her, sending her plunging into another, deeper orgasm.

Her entire body shook, flashes of light shot from her body. Black thrust once more and groaned out her name as he came, his body locking with hers, his light shining like a thousand golden suns.

They stayed joined together, so intimately, for only moments more. They were both breathing hard, and the light gently faded with each beat of their hearts. When he pulled away, Kady tightened her legs, not letting him go, just yet.

"Just a little bit longer," she whispered.

"Forever."

He kissed her, taking her mouth, in a deep, soul deep, way. When he unlocked their lips, he did the same for their bodies. She groaned, protesting, but he rolled them both, so she lay in his arms.

They drifted to sleep that way, linked by more than Kady ever imagined was possible.

Not so quiet whispers outside the bedroom door woke her in the morning. Black was gone, and the bed was cold.

She reached for her clothes, and remembered she only had a towel. Well, damn.

"Dear Universe." Man, she felt dumb, but if she had some sort of magical powers, at least it could cloth her.

"Dear Universe, please help me out with some clothes." With only the words and a thought, they were on her body. She been thinking they would manifest where her towel had been or something. She hadn't been trying to put them on, she'd just wished she was already dressed. Then poof, she was.

She'd need to learn to tightly control that particular part of her magic, or she and Black would be naked all the damn time.

"I think we need to wake her. It was her magic that brought them."

"You don't know that. Maybe it was her magic that kept them at bay."

The Gundersons were arguing. Kady stuck her head out of the room. Margreth was futzing about in the kitchenette and Sigar was pacing. She didn't see Black anywhere.

"I don't suppose you could show me how to manifest some coffee, could you?"

Margreth smacked her husband on the arm and gave him the shut-your-pie-hole look. "No need, dear. I have some all ready for you. Figured you'd need it after your fireworks show last night."

Kady turned forty-nine shades of pink. They had seen that?

She took the coffee, which already had a ton of cream and sugar, exactly how she liked it, and took several gulps to hide her embarrassment.

"Your bear is waiting outside for you. We'd better go take a look with him."

What were they looking at?

The sun shone, and the sky sparkled a deep blue. In fact, it sparkled too much. All across the sky, just above the trees, black and blue cracks, like spider-webbing in a broken windshield fizzled.

Black stood a few feet away, wearing only his torn pants, staring up at the cracks in the sky. His arms were folded, and hard lines crossed his face. Concentration and worry were marred by his frown.

"Black? What are those? It looks like the sky is cracked." Kady stepped beside him and stared up to the same place he looked.

"It's not the sky, but the protective wards the gnomes have set up around their garden. They form a dome shape. What you're seeing is the damage caused by attempts to break through their wards."

"By the TFO?"

"No. Something much worse."

9

SPECTRAL STORM

"Tell me again what you think you saw." Black paced on the grass alternating between staring at the cracks in the wards and the gnomes that had placed them.

"Well, I came outside when I saw the lights out our window. Wanted to check that you all were safe." Sigar stroked his beard.

Margreth touched his nose. "You old perv, you knew they were fine. You wanted to see their fireworks."

"So, what if I did? Anyway, while you two were lighting up the sky, I caught something out of the corner of my eye."

Black had never experienced anything like what had happened between him and Kady last night. He'd heard that sex between mates was different, he'd thought simply better, more intense. He hadn't expected her to pull his soul from his body and dance with it.

The fireworks the Gundersons had thought they were watching was the carnal dance of his soul blending with Kady's.

He'd been so close to completing their mating, biting her, marking her, and claiming her for all the galaxy to know that she was his. He'd barely been able to resist fusing their souls for all time.

He had to complete his mission, defeat the spectral warriors, before he could take the time to go back to the crash site and try to recover his soul ember. Until then the two of them couldn't be united.

"What did you see?" Black was already sure he knew. There was too much evidence to be anything else.

Sigar continued. "I don't rightly know. I've never seen anything like it before. They were like ghosts, but not any spooks I've known."

"I know this is going to sound like a dumb question, but are ghosts real?" His sweet Kady had so much to learn about who she was and where she belonged.

He loved watching as she uncovered each new discovery. Her awe and wonder at the parts of his world that were banal breathed new life into him. Gave him hope.

And hope was a dangerous thing for a soldier like him to have.

"Yes, dear. But these weren't ghosts. They were eerie, like they were made of both darkness and shadow, the very opposite of light." Margreth shivered and rubbed her arms trying to stave off a chill that wasn't there.

Sigar pointed to the cracks in the sky. "They bombarded the wards. I've never seen wards get a visible crack."

Black wished Electra had sent him and his team to Earth sooner, maybe even contacted Star Marine Niko's mate about these protective wards. The only thing that had ever held the

Spectral Warriors at bay, had been condensate matter reinforced graphene of a meter or thicker. It was difficult to produce and could only be made in small quantities. Not even the coalition had the resources to manufacture enough to create a barrier around an area as big as the Gundersons' field. Even if they did, it wouldn't last even a tenth of the time these wards had.

"I even tried reinforcing them, but it doesn't seem to make a difference."

Because the spectrals would sacrifice and destroy themselves in pursuit of their target. What they were all seeing in the sky wasn't just the cracks in the wards, it was chunks of the spectrals themselves, left like blood from an injury.

It was the same as he'd seen at the graphene plant that had been attacked and destroyed. He'd needed his spectral visor to see the remains there.

What Black didn't understand was why they could see the spectrals or their remains with the bare eye now.

"The more light the two of you put out, the more they attacked the wards. Those buggers did not like your fireworks, pretty witch."

Kady appeared visibly shaken. She could figure out how to defend herself, and him, against other humans, but she hadn't embraced her own powers or that of the rest of the world around her. He saw in the way her hands shook when she sipped from her mug that the idea of an attack of this kind, scared her.

She should be scared. The spectral warriors scared him. They were pure mindless evil, and a scourge on the galaxy.

He'd been a Star Marine for a long time, and even the

worst of the worst had a motivation for why they killed, maimed, attacked, or destroyed those around them. But not the spectral warriors, not that he could understand.

They were emotionless, voiceless, driven only by stealing another soul and leaving behind an empty husk, still living, but completely void.

He'd seen it firsthand. His own homeworld of Honaw had been devastated by the spectrals. They'd stolen the lives of those dear to him.

He would never let them steal Kady.

He would die himself, first.

"Sigar, you said yesterday you needed to transport the abode we stayed in. I suggest you prepare it and leave. The spectral warriors will continue to attack until they break through your wards."

"Oh no. Not our little garden." Margreth hugged Sigar and glanced around the area as if committing it all the memory, knowing today was the last time she'd see it.

"Kady and I must continue on to our destination, so I can hook up with my team and use this new information to work to defeat this blight on the galaxy."

Sigar patted his wife's back. "Where is your team, bear?"

"Rogue, New York. There is another Star Marine there who will be able to help us." Niko and his witch mate Zara should be able to help with the spectrals and Kady's formidable but budding powers.

"Then that's where we're going too. Margreth has a cousin who runs the taxi service in Rogue. They'll take us in."

"Good. How long do you need to prepare?" Black wanted to be underway as soon as they could.

"Not long, maybe a couple hours. We need to prepare and load the other containers on the truck."

He nodded, and the gnomes hurried off. That gave him enough time to teach Kady to defend herself.

She stood off to the side, looking lost and alone. He wanted nothing more than to wrap her up in layers of graphene lined with the softest down and protect her.

Not only did he not have that luxury, he didn't think Kady would want it that way. She'd already proven she was smart and resourceful, that she could keep a level head in a dangerous situation.

That was fucking hot. His curvy warrior princess had his soul burning for her and his cock twitching. He crossed to her and ran his hands through her soft hair.

"Black, I heard the Gundersons talking this morning. They think my magic brought those things here." Kady twirled her mug in her hands and stared down at the ground.

The Star Marines didn't know enough about the spectrals to know when and where they would strike. "I have had many run ins with them, so it's more likely they were here for me."

"But how would they know you were here?"

This part he didn't want to tell her. "The spectrals are soul stealers. They have had a taste of my soul before, so when we made love and our souls danced around us, they were probably drawn to it."

"Holy crap. We are never having sex again. I don't want anything to steal your soul."

Black pulled Kady to him, holding her tight to his body. "Oh, we will have lots of sex, *mah wah*."

He kissed her, letting her taste the truth of his words. He could take her right there, in the field, but not before teaching her to fend off the spectrals.

He left her panting, and wanting, the soft glow of her soul seeking his across her skin. Exactly how he wished he could keep her. "But first, let's play with your powers. You can use them to keep yourself safe."

Black had known witches on his world, but he only partly knew how their magic worked. They were nothing compared to Kady. Mostly he knew of healers who could do tricks that helped them in their trade, like spurring plant growth, making small objects appear or disappear, and mixing potions. The strongest magic he'd ever seen was when a witch and taken a sliver of his soul and bound it in his ember.

What he did understand was that a similar energy fueled the bear inside of him. He'd had to learn how to harness that as a cub crossing into adulthood, and he hoped the same idea would help Kady seize her own abilities.

"Can I use them to keep you safe too?"

"We'll see. Now close your eyes. I want you to think of the last time you noticed your magic working."

Kady scrunched her eyes tight and wrinkled her nose. "Okay, I got it."

She concentrated so hard, and her face was adorable like this. He should tell her to relax and let the magic flow, but he was getting a kick out of seeing her concentrate so hard.

"Good, where do you feel it in your body?"

"I think it's behind my heart, but kind of in my throat and belly too."

"Concentrate on that feeling, breathe into it."

Kady's face relaxed with each breath and the glow of her skin increased. Not in the same way as before, this light was all her own. Soft, ethereal, and a deep amber.

It reminded him of the color of his soul ember. He reached for the pendant that he'd hadn't been without since he became a man. It still wasn't there. Without it, he couldn't complete the mating, couldn't claim her fully, and make her his forever.

"I feel it. It's soft and warm."

"See if you can expand it, let it spread across your whole body."

The amber glow swelled, washing across her skin, surrounding her in its light.

"Yes, that's it, love. Your magic is as beautiful as you."

Kady opened her eyes and they wandered, looking at the waves of light and energy pouring out of her. "It is pretty. But what can I do with it?"

"You'll learn more than I can teach you when we get to New York. For now, see if you can turn the soft light into something hard, like a shield."

Kady closed her eyes again. Her light shimmered, and she disappeared.

Black reached out, searching for her, and found her arm. She was there, but invisible. Where his hand touched her, it faded as well. That was a damn good trick.

"Don't open your eyes, but concentrate on that feeling, right there. Hold it, feel it, so you can try to recreate it."

Her voice was soft, but confident. "Is it the shield, like you said?"

"No. But this is even better. Do you have the feeling?

Think you can do it again?" He would make her practice until she could.

"Maybe."

"Come back to that warm soft place you found before." Kady shimmered back into view.

As she reappeared her soft light pushed out from her, expanding, turning from a glow to rays of light. The light reached up to the sky penetrating the remaining wards.

A high-pitched scream, like a fighter ship tearing through the sky mixed with the call of a banshee, screeched through the air.

Black looked up and saw the spectral bearing down, crash into the wards, cracking it even further.

"Kady, pull back your light, now."

She gasped and instead of her light coming back to her, it spread like an explosion through the sky. The spectral screamed again at first reaching for her light, then recoiling as it crackled, burned by her magic. It didn't stay away long, hurtling itself at both her light and the wards.

"Ouch. Ow." Kady cried out, matching the pain of the creature.

Black pulled her to him, took her face in his hands. Her light sizzled through him too, but it didn't hurt, it washed through him like the energy of a thousand men. "*Mah wah,* relax, bring your light back, back to me. Close your eyes and find that feeling you had before."

"Ouch, I can't." Kady's eyes darted from the spectral that was attacking her light, to him, and back again.

"You can Kady, you must."

She swallowed and nodded her head. Her eyes fluttered shut, but her face jerked as the spectral continued its barrage.

The sky above them shattered. The wards were destroyed. The spectral plummeted through the air toward them.

Fates above, please don't take her from me now.

He added hope to his prayer that his next move would work. That he could help her be safe.

Black kissed her, rolling her to the ground, and under him. He swept his tongue into her mouth, and let his soul rise to mingle with her.

Kady grasped at him, shoving her hands into his hair and kissed him back, taking as much as she was giving.

If they were both about to lose their souls to this spectral, there was no other way he'd rather go.

Kady's light shimmered and the world around them faded away. It was as if she was bending the light around them. No that wasn't quite right. She was slowing the light, dissipating it, scattering it.

They could still hear the scream of the spectral and in the next instant it was upon them. Black waited for his soul to be ripped from his body, he wished for Kady that it be fast and painless.

The spectral warrior passed into the slowed light space around them, and Black saw a face he knew, would always remember, would never forget.

"Mother?"

10

WARRIOR WITCH

Kady had no idea what she was doing, she only knew the thing that attacked couldn't hurt them anymore.

The being had burst through the shield Black had told her to call up. This time she understood what to do, where the magic came from deep inside of her, and she'd expanded the shield to encompass them both, protecting them together.

When it passed through the barrier a thousand needles poked at her from the inside out.

Kady clearly saw the being, a dark shadowy liquid mercury, that reminded her of an angry genie out of its bottle. Almost as fast as it penetrated her shield, it began to dissipate, the fluid transforming into wisps of nothingness.

"Mother?" Black whispered, both pain and surprise lacing the word like poison.

The last part of the being to dissolve before their eyes was the face of an older woman, lines of pain, smeared with... what?

Sadness and relief.

"Kady, Black, are you two okay?" The Gundersons scurried to the part of the field she and Black were lying in.

Kady wasn't quite ready to release her shield and the Gundersons ran right past them. She held Black tightly, partly for herself, but mostly because he'd gone as still as an ice statue.

Had that creature been his mother? Talk about a monster-in-law.

"Black." Kady stroked his face and whispered to him.

A muscle ticked in his jaw and he continued to stare, or glare at the spot where the being, his mother, had disappeared.

"Come back to me now." She whispered again and this time he heard her.

He blinked and let go of the breath he'd been holding. "Good work using your magic to defend us from the spectral warrior."

This wasn't her Black. The voice was distant and curt. The meaning behind the words sincere, but as if they were what he was expected to say.

This Black was a detached soldier.

He got to his feet and his action broke the shield. The only concession to indicate the man she'd made love to, was falling in love with, might already be in love with, was a hand to help her up.

"Black?" What was she supposed to say? Are you okay, didn't even begin to cover it. If that was really his mother, there was a whole lot more going on here than she understood.

Hadn't he said his mother had a farm?

Kady knew Black's mission had to do with hunting down the spectral warriors and that he and his team needed to find a way to defeat them.

The spectrals were the bad guys. That thing had been part of the Dark Side, that she knew.

Chills ran down her neck and up her jaw. What if this was like a Skywalker family reunion. Instead of Luke, I am your father, it was Black, I am your mother.

He didn't respond to her at all, but instead walked across the field toward the houses. The Gundersons spun on their heels when they saw him and started trucking back.

They had to pass her to get to him and stopped to gather her along.

"You've got some powerful magic, pretty witch. Disappearing like that." Margreth wagged her finger.

Kady frowned. Disappearing? "I just put up a shield that Black taught me."

"Your shield made you invisible and injured the creature. We saw it dissipate, then reform, but it was weaker, both in form and energy."

"It's still here?" She ducked, hoping it wasn't already attacking.

Sigar pointed to the hole in the sky that still glowed around the edges. "No, no, it flew back out the hole it had crashed through the wards." He shook his head and tsked. "It was really gunning for you. Lucky you learned that shield or I think the two of you would be in a sorry state."

She had learned more than a shield. Her magic had injured the spectral. If Black could help her learn more, maybe she could use it as a weapon instead.

She'd show those bully spectrals who was a badass.

Then maybe she could help Black and his team fight against them. She could stand up for the meek since no one had ever stood up for her.

Except Black. He'd risked his life to save hers during the TFO attack, and he'd thrown himself between her and the attacking spectral. Her warrior bear had been ready to sacrifice himself for her.

If she had her way, he wouldn't have to sacrifice ever again. She was done hiding from the world, trying to avoid the mean and scary things in the universe, letting them win.

Kady had her own powers now. She didn't know exactly how they worked or what they could and couldn't do. But she knew with Black by her side she had a fighting chance for the first time in her life.

Now to convince him.

Black had retreated to where the container tiny homes had been, although only the one they had stayed in was still in the field. She couldn't imagine what they Gundersons had done with the other ones, but that last container come tiny house was now on a trailer, and her truck, Herbie, was on a smaller trailer behind it.

Kady jogged across the field, her mind running through all the ways she could help Black's team. She could throw up the shield around them all, she could learn to focus the shield into a sword...or a light saber.

She was definitely going to need Jedi robes, or a super suit. But no cape. Capes were dangerous. Nothing spandex with stars and stripes was going anywhere near her butt either.

She found Black pacing, back and forth, back and forth, saying something under his breath. Swearing up a storm.

He didn't seem to notice her, so she reached out and touched his arm. He jumped about a yard and the form of the bear shimmered for a moment.

He clenched his fists and took several deep breaths, the bear receded. He paced once again, angry energy shooting off him. "Kady. I'm sorry for fucking leaving you open and vulnerable like that. I'm an ass and shouldn't have. You are mine to protect now."

She didn't need protecting so much anymore. "Maybe you're mine to protect."

Black stopped his pacing, grabbed her up and laid a good hard kiss on her. This wasn't a possessive kiss, he had a need, some vulnerability.

Kady kissed him back, just as fiercely, trying to let him know she was there for him. He'd had a pretty harsh shock and she wanted to soothe him, take care of him.

The warm glow that came from deep inside of her surfaced and she concentrated on spreading it to Black, wrapping them both in its heat.

A shriek sounded from far above them, forcing them to break apart.

Margreth snagged her arm and pulled her toward their container house. Sigar did the same with Black. "Come on you two, inside. We've put up wards around the house, so it should hold those nasty beings off for a little while."

The four of them ran inside, and Sigar slammed the door behind them. Margreth waved her arms and said some words

Kady didn't recognize. A flash zipped through the building and then a series of crashes and screeches came from outside.

"The spectrals are attacking again. In force this time." Black looked out the window at the exact moment something crashed into it. The glass remained untouched, but a small spider web of cracks formed a few centimeters off the side of the window.

Black slammed his hand against the wall, bear claws extending from the ends of his fingers. "Fuck. I can't do a goddamned thing to fight them."

She hated seeing Black feel so helpless. What she was about to say might make him feel even more so. She hoped not. But she had to take the chance. For the first time in her life, she not only could do something to fight against the bad guys, she wanted to.

"I can." At first her voice was only a whisper, but her soul wanted to shout. "I can fight them with my magic."

11

SEX MAGIC

A deep cut ached in the pit of Black's stomach. He shook his head, denying her words. No way could he put Kady into battle with the spectrals. The Fates had both blessed and cursed him with a mate as amazing as his curvy little witch. He wasn't worthy of her.

She was soft and tender, and oh so fierce. It would kill him, tear his soul from his body to lose her. More than losing his mother to the spectral warriors.

The crashing against the wards continued while Black pushed against Kady's idea.

"Let the witch try, bear. She may be our only hope."

The Gundersons held each other, their wards the only thing standing between the spectrals and a fate worse than death.

Black had thought his mother was lost to him forever. Only a shell of her former self remained. She lived, she breathed, she could perform the most menial of tasks, but she was a blank shell. The bastards had stolen her being.

Kady had shown him what happened to his mother's soul.

He swallowed hard, and pulled Kady into his arms, holding her tight against his chest.

"I can do it, Black. I need to try."

She had done something that neither he, his elite team, nor any others battling the scourge had been able to figure out how to do. She had injured the enemy.

Up until now they had only been able to track the spectrals with the most advanced technology the Marine force could come up with.

Every weapon they'd tried, plasma weapons, lasers, disruptors, phasors, hadn't done anything to even slow the bastards down. Too many souls had already been lost to them.

Kady and her magic could be the first step in winning the war, to saving the galaxy. It also drew them to her. Her bright shining soul, and her magic was like nectar to them.

What if he lost her too?

If it were only about himself, he would gladly sacrifice to save millions. It was the life he'd chosen, to serve, so that others could live.

She had not made that choice. She was the one he'd signed up to defend.

He was faced with the hardest decision he could ever imagine. None of his training had prepared him for this.

Save the galaxy or save the love of his life, and his soul.

Only if the Fates smiled on him, could he have both. He said a silent prayer, thanking them for bringing her into his life, and asking for their help and benevolence.

"Okay, *mah wah,* let's go save the world." He took one last opportunity to savor having her in his arms and kissed the top of her head. Then he switched into commando mode.

"Sigar, are you ready to transport your containers?"

The gnome nodded. "All the rest are miniaturized and loaded. I had a devil of a time getting the broom loaded onto the trailer, but it's there too."

"Herbie? My truck?"

Sigar nodded.

One down, a thousand more details to go to make the plan Black was building on the fly happen. "And the transport?"

"The big rig is ready, but we need to hook her up to the trailer.

"Margreth, what can you do to reinforce the wards, anything?"

"I've used up all the simple spells I can do." She shook her head. "But this ward is just around the container, so it's stronger, more solid because it doesn't have to stretch to cover the whole garden. It should hold longer than the last one."

"That's good. Do you have a way to contact your cousin? I need to get through to my team."

"Yes, I can call him, but not with the wards up. Nothing is going in or out."

"That's okay, just be prepared. We'll contact him on our way."

The Gundersons nodded and clasped hands, standing together against the threat to their home and lives. "We're ready for whatever you need us to do."

Black admired how these two little gnomes were proudly

ready to fight. They were good additions to his temporary team.

But his mate was the lynchpin in the whole plan. He took her hand. "Kady, are you ready to try something new with your magic?"

"Yes. I think I understand where it comes from now. What's your plan?"

"We are going on the offensive. We're going to fight our way to Rogue, New York."

"Won't that be bringing the spectrals to them?"

"We need to regroup with my team and get reinforcements. There's a pack of wolves in Rogue who we've joined forces with to fight against the scourge. The alpha's mate also has powers. I'm hoping they can either help by utilizing her and any other witches in the area, or that she can help you focus your power."

"Okay. So, we get to Rogue, and then we can bring the fight to the bad guys. I like that. What do you want me to do?"

"I need you to turn your power outward, instead of shield, we need—"

"A sword?"

"An explosion."

Kady looked surprised and her eyes flitted back and forth, processing what he needed her to do. "I think I can do that. I don't totally get how to control it, but maybe that's a good thing right now. It feels a bit explosive when it let it out anyway." She grinned up at him, almost shyly. "The magic is stronger when we're together. So, you'll have to help me."

"That is the only part of this plan I like." He couldn't help letting his eyes fall to her lips.

For the first time in as long as he could remember, Black wished for another life. One where he didn't have to serve and protect but could live simply and grow old with Kady.

He'd get it in as much loving her as he could, while he could. They hadn't completed the mating, their souls had danced, touched, played, but they hadn't become one.

Even if the Fates and the mating drive were pushing the two of them together as hard as they possibly could, he wanted to allow her to choose. Choose him.

If he had to sacrifice himself to save her, she would survive. Because there was no way he would let Kady die. He would have to ask his brothers to care for her, be there through her loneliest dark hours.

Kady was strong. A life without a mate was hard, but she had such a fire in her that she would be okay. He had to make himself believe.

Not that he was going anywhere if he could help it. Black kissed Kady, long and hard. She melted into his arms, giving everything he wanted to take, taking everything he wanted to give.

Their souls mingled and Kady's magic teased, making his skin tingle. Without having to open his eyes, he knew they were lighting up the room and beyond.

Crashes shook the container, the spectrals reacting to the draw her magic had on them. Still he kissed her. This wasn't for the magic, their defense. This kiss was for him. Something to take into the upcoming battle.

Kady wrapped her hands into his hair, holding him tight,

like she too knew this might be their only chance to be together. The air around them pulsed with the energy from her magic and their souls.

He pressed his hips forward, showing Kady the affect she had on his body. He was hard as graphene and ready to take her now, on the floor.

She moaned into his mouth and reached for his pants. He couldn't let her. He wanted her to be the one aroused. In the short time they had, he'd have to play a good game of fore.

Black lifted Kady, helping her wrap her legs around his waist. Thank Fates this living space was so damn small, so the wall was only a few steps away. He pushed her back against it, letting her slide down far enough that his hard cock pressed right at the apex of her sex.

Even through their clothes he felt her heat, her need. It matched his own. He didn't have time to strip her and dry humping against the wall could only take them so far.

If only he could complete the mating. Bite her neck, claim her and her soul. But he had nothing to give in return, not without his soul ember.

He couldn't resist trying anyway. Black grabbed Kady's chin and turned her head to the side, baring her neck and shoulder to him. He kissed the soft skin above her collar bone apologizing in advance for marring it.

"Whoo, boy. That feels amazing. More, do it more." Even Kady's body knew the power this bite, his mark would have on their souls. A powerful beam of light emanated from her, throwing a million sparks into the air.

He scraped his teeth across her skin and licked to soothe the marks he made.

"Oh, god, yes, Black, yes." She bucked beneath him, pulling them both close to coming.

Black drug himself away from her skin, from the siren call to make her his forever, only far enough to whisper against her ear. "Hold that energy, don't let it go, yet."

She licked her lips and drug her teeth across the bottom one. She nodded and held her breath, concentrating. The effort to bank her magic was tough on her. Golden light swirled through her eyes, along with passion.

"Good girl. Draw on that lust, hold onto it for now, and I promise to bring it back to you tenfold when we are safe."

Kady drew in two deep breaths and nodded ever so slightly. She was barely containing her magic. Black needed to act fast to put the first phase of this plan into action.

"When I say go, take all you have, *mah wah*, and throw it out in every direction. Hit them hard, for me." He gave her luscious ass a final squeeze making it the same promise of returning for pleasure, set her feet on the floor, and bolted across the room.

"Sigar, we have to make a mad dash to get the transport and the trailer attached as soon as Kady blasts them. Ready?"

Sigar nodded and gave his wife's hand one last squeeze.

"Margreth, when I say go, release your wards. Kady will blast them and we'll run for the transport."

She didn't look convinced she should do as he asked. "You're sure it will work, that it will be safe?"

The building shook again, and the trailer it sat on tilted. It was now or never. "No, but I believe in Kady. Look after her once Sigar and I are on the move."

Black took one final cleansing breath, focused his mind

and shouted the order to go, adding a final plea to the Fates to help them all survive.

Kady shimmered and disappeared before their eyes and Black took that as his signal to grab up Sigar and run.

Two steps out the door, and they saw the mass of spectral warriors lined up around the container. They didn't notice him or Sigar, their focus wholly on the area where Kady was inside. She hadn't yet released the wave of power Black had been hoping she could.

"There, in the trees, that's where the rig is hidden." Sigar pointed to a large vehicle hidden by a few branches about fifty meters away.

They could easily make it there in under ten seconds. That would also be enough time for the spectrals to slide right through the metal walls of the container and steal the souls of both Margreth and Kady.

Why hadn't she released her magic yet. If he ran now he might draw them away, but probably not. He also wouldn't be able to protect her.

Fuck.

"Kady, now, *mah wah*. Now, go go go."

His shouts attracted the attention of half a dozen of the spectrals. Good. Less of them to focus on her.

If he ran for the vehicle now they might follow him and bring more along. That also meant running away from Kady.

He would never forgive himself if this didn't work.

Black shouted to Kady again to blast them and then took off at his top speed toward the vehicle. He called upon his bear to give him all its strength and stamina.

The bear inside let out a roar and pushed forth, shimmering as near to the shift without fully taking over.

They were ten meters from reaching their destination when two men in the same black suits and dark glasses stepped from the trees and blocked their path. Two spectral warriors hovered inches above and behind them, baring a striking resemblance to the men.

Black barreled toward them, hoping to take out the men in his path. The spectrals rose up, were joined by at least ten more of their kind and screeched down on Black and Sigar.

Sigar cried out, raising his arms in front of his face. Black pivoted to the right, stepped around the men and dove for the cockpit of the vehicle. He tossed Sigar through the air like a fallenball, praying for a goal.

A spectral warrior turned and attacked Sigar, mere inches from the gnome. The rest of the spectrals bore down on Black. He could do nothing to stop them but could try to take out the men in black along the way.

He allowed the shift to overtake him and the bear tore free, fur and claws bursting forth, ready for the fight. His clawed paws struck through the first man, severing his head from his body, and he sank his teeth into the jugular of the second.

The spectral warriors, stolen from the pair, flickered, and disappeared into a puff of scattered light.

Black wanted the time to consider the implications of what had just happened before his eyes, and relay the information to his team, his brothers, but ten more spectrals soared toward him, and in less than a second, he would either be dead, or worse.

The only thing he could do now was send his love out into the world for Kady and ask her forgiveness that they didn't have more time together.

Whoosh.

A brilliant golden explosion lit up the land, the sky, the trees, and his soul.

Mere millimeters from his chest, the spectral who'd been about to steal his soul, was obliterated, it's light scattering just as the ones he'd killed.

His Kady had saved them all.

He and Sigar glanced at each other and then at the house. Damn, that had been close.

Black took a deep breath, willing the bear back down so he could find his mate and spank her ass for waiting so long to release her magic.

Then he'd take her back into the bedroom and see what he could do to beat their six-orgasm record.

Mid-shift, his bear refused to be contained. Which could only mean one thing. They were all still in danger.

Black ran back toward the container, searching for the threat. Nothing. The field was clear, the trees, empty.

He had to get to Kady. Find her, warn her, protect her.

A scream wrenched through the air. Kady's scream.

12

KEY TO VICTORY

Blood dripped down Kady's fingers and onto the floor. The fucking bastard had cut her. He would have sliced into her face if she hadn't blocked him.

"I told you there would be consequences if you tried anything." The same man who'd blustered his way into her bath house hovered over her now.

"You're the douchecanoe who is going to be facing consequences." She didn't know what those were yet because she'd tried to magic him to death, and all it had done was put a few icicles in his hair.

She needed Black to come help recharge her magic. Then she'd freeze this TFO bully's balls off.

"As soon as my back-up gets here, we are taking you in. You'll never see the light of day again for destroying months of work."

The front door crashed in and the biggest most beautiful black bear snarled in douchcanoe's direction.

"Ha. Here are those consequences I told you about." She kicked out, catching the TFO man in the knee.

He lost his balance and his knife-like weapon went clattering to the floor. Black took the opportunity to lunge, but his great size in the little space put him at a disadvantage. The dude rolled, narrowly evading Black's claws, which cut right through the floorboards.

Kady snatched up the knife-weapon, that wasn't a knife at all. It vibrated in her hand and was cold to the touch. It might not be a knife, but it had cut her, so it could hurt douchecanoe too.

Before she could throw it, or stab at him, Black put his big ole bear butt between her and the bully. That left the doorway open and he escaped from the container and Black's wrath.

Black charged after him, but by the time they got outside, straight out of a spy movie, a helicopter swooped down and dropped a rope ladder. Their nasty enemy climbed, signaling the crew to pull him up.

He pointed toward them, rather ominously, as the chopper flew away.

Black's sides and chest expanded and huffed. He was breathing hard and a snarl rumbled low in his throat.

Jiminy Christmas he was big. The last time he'd shifted they'd been getting shot at and fleeing for their lives and she hadn't really gotten to see him in all his beary glory.

She touched the fur on his shoulder and he turned on her, snapping at her hand. He was still deep in protective bear mode, but she wasn't even a little bit afraid.

He continued to huff and puff, rocking back and forth on his front legs like he had too much angry energy.

Kady smiled, loving this big bad side of him. She shouldn't. The alpha male rumbling represented all that had always scared her. He was cranky, and big, and cranky, and male, and cranky, and could hurt her like most every other big bad man in her life had.

Because she'd let them. She hadn't known what was inside of her, and she didn't mean her magic. Sure, that helped, but pushed to the brink, tested and tried by an alien ship crash, a covert government agency, and some weird ass spectral warrior monsters, she'd withstood. In fact, she'd thrived.

A cranky bear, who she loved, yeah, that's right loved, didn't scare her one bit.

Kady reached out and held Black's muzzle between her hands. She stroked the soft fur on his face, looking into his eyes, the same ones that she saw in the man, and softly called his name. "Black, come back to me now."

He huffed one more time, but then his form shimmered and soon she held the man's face.

He grabbed her in his arms, lifting her under the knees and carried her back into the house. He was heading back toward the bedroom again and with the adrenaline of that last battle still coursing through her system, a good ole romp in the hay sounded like a great idea.

"Black, wait. Stop. Margreth is hurt too."

He didn't stop. "Sigar can care for her."

"No. She was trying to protect me. Put me down. There will be time for some nookie later."

Black growled but set her down. "We will be nookie-ing as soon as you tend to Margreth. I need you in my arms, under me, crying my name as I make you come. I need to know that you are okay."

Aww. That made her heart go pitter-skip-patter. "I know, I want to feel you inside of me, and know that you're okay too. Let's make sure our gnomes are okay, and get the hell out of here."

Black stared at her for a few moments and then nodded. He took her hand and gently touched the wound. "I'll go help Sigar finish hooking up the trailer to his vehicle. You tend to yourself and Margreth."

He kissed her hand and then went outside. Kady found Margreth sitting on a stump in the yard. She had Percy in her lap and was stroking his belly.

"Percy. I wondered where you'd gone off to. I'm glad you're okay." Kady tapped Percy's little nose, happy her tiny friend wasn't injured.

Margreth smiled and handed him over to her. "Little thing was biting at the pant leg of one of our evil friends. He's a tough little familiar."

Percy crawled up Kady's arm, nuzzled her neck and then disappeared into her sleeve. "Are you okay? Were you hurt?"

The TFO man had tossed Margreth out of his way like a rag doll. That man ranked right up there with Darth Mal if you asked her.

"Oh, I'll have a bruise or two, but we gnomes are built solid. I'm fine. We should have a look at your hand though."

They bandaged her cut and picked up the broken furniture and bits of the door and doorjamb that had gotten broken in the fracas.

The trailer jolted as Sigar and Black got it hooked up to the truck tractor. Then they both popped back inside.

Kady eyed the truck through the broken front door. "I don't know where you kept that big rig hidden all this time."

Sigar laughed. "Oh, there's these funny youngins, twins Ellie and Tristan. Back in Rogue they gave us a miniaturization spell. They are big pranksters, those two, thought it was funny to turn each other gnome sized. We've been using it ever since to transport the tiny houses we make."

Margreth joined her husband, pecking him on the cheek. "Speaking of transport. We'd better get this truck on the road. Now that the wards are down, we can call my cousin and get you connected with your team."

They all worked on the final preparations. Sigar nailed a tarp over the broken door, while Margreth moved the truck and trailer to the hidden entrance to the road.

"Roger that. The Reserve parking lot. We'll meet you there in approximately thirty Earth hours." Black punched the button to hang up the iPhone Margreth had loaned him.

"I thought maybe they'd, umm, fly up here and get you." Kady had begun to worry about how long she and Black still had together. Would he go back to his job in space without her when they got to New York?

"No. Electra, our commander, has sent down some orders in my absence. She's had Titian set up a base for us to work from in Rogue. My brothers are tracking a lead on a group of spectral soldiers in a placed called Three Mile Island, and

Fedelis will be working to infiltrate the TFO. Everyone needs time to work on their tasks."

"Do you have a task?"

"Indeed, I do, my curvy witch." Black's voice had jumped down an octave and he stalked toward her.

Kady's heart revved, excited by the lust in Black's eyes. "What do you have to do?"

He backed her up against the wall and caged her in with his arms. "My part of the mission is key to defeating the spectral scourge."

Her breathing joined in the race with her heart, competing to see which could go faster. "It is? How are you going to do that?"

He leaned in and nibbled at Kady's earlobe. "You and I have learned more information about them, and how to destroy them in the past two days, than my team and the entire force of the Marines has been able to in a year."

"That's good. I'm glad I could help." She ran her fingers along the back of Black's neck, wanting to tease him as much as he was teasing her.

"It's very good. I've been tasked with making sure you learn to wield your magic. Help you learn to control it."

"Mmm-hmm."

"You and I both know how to build your powers up, to make them want to burst from deep inside of you."

"Oh, yes, we do."

Sigar cleared his throat. "Ahem."

Oops. She'd completely forgotten he was still in the room.

"We're set to go. You'll be more comfortable riding in the container house, than in the cab with me and Margreth." He unhooked one corner of the tarp and stepped outside. "Maybe you two can call up some of Kady's magic to shield us on our drive to New York while you're at it. I don't think those TFO folks and their spooks are going to just let us truck on down the road."

"Okay, we'll work on that," Kady called.

"Yes, let's work on that. Right now." Black stripped her shirt right up and off her. He tossed it, and Percy on the couch.

"I don't think I've paid nearly enough attention to these fucking amazing tits of yours." Black cupped his hands over her bra and lifted her breasts.

Kady wiggled her nose and in a blink the bra was gone. His skin to hers tingled and burned in a lovely way.

He stroked his thumbs across her nipples and the telltale glow of arousal sparkled across her chest.

"Yes, *mah wah*, show me your soul. Harness the feeling, understand how my touch calls to your body, to your magic." He lowered his head and licked one nipple and then sucked the other into his mouth.

A burst of light flooded the room when he did that. "Ooh, Black, that feels so good. I love it when you do that."

He bit at her sensitive skin before letting her breast fall from his mouth. "I'll do it all night, but you must focus on how it brings up your power."

Kady closed her eyes, imagined having Black touch her, pleasure her, and pushed the feeling out and around them.

"Yes, Kady. Good." Black unbuckled her pants and pulled them down her legs, following them.

Kady helped him the rest of the way by making her undies go the way of her bra.

"Fates above, I love these lush thighs of yours." He kissed one, and then the other, working his way from above her knee to her pussy.

Kady had never particularly liked her thick thighs, except maybe that one time they had caught her cell phone and kept it from falling into the toilet. But with each of Black's licks, nips, and kisses, she grew to like them more and more.

"Your dark curls call to me. Look how your plump pussy is already wet. It's begging to be licked."

"Yes, please." How could he keep talking at a time like this? She needed his mouth on her now.

"I'm going to lick, and suck, and even bite your sweet pussy, but if you don't focus your power, I'll stop, my love."

"Oh, that's not fair. How would you like it if I said you had to fly your spaceship while I sucked on your dick?"

Yeah. She'd blurted that out.

Black stood up so fast, she didn't even have time to blink. He pushed his fingers between her legs and stroked across her clit. "Focus your power now, and I'll be sure to let you try your seductive little plan just as soon as we get to a ship."

"I'm going to hold you to that." Actually, at the moment, she didn't care at all. She only wanted Black inside of her, pushing them both to orgasm.

"Push the field you have around the two of us, out. Wrap it around the transport." He pinched at, pulled at her clit, driving her crazy.

"I can't focus with your fingers doing that."

He stroked her faster, pushing her higher. "You must. Your magic, this thing between us, draws them. If you don't focus, and create your shield to protect us, we won't make it to New York."

No pressure.

"Kiss me, Black." She took several gulps. "I can do it, if you kiss me."

13

WELCOME TO ROGUE

Could he kiss her? The question was could he stop kissing her.

Never.

Black had to work to focus himself. Yes, he wanted to love on Kady, bring her pleasure, hear her call his name as she came. He also had to help her understand how to control her magic and the power she could wield with it.

She may be their only hope.

If he could help her contain her power, they could evade the enemy and she could learn to wield it against them strategically.

He continued to slide his fingers through her pussy. He wanted to bury his cock in her wet heat more than he wanted his next breath. But not more than he wanted Kady to have hers.

He would deny himself to help her learn to save herself.

She may be the only way to save the galaxy. Control of her power was the only thing that could protect her from the scourge too. "Turn your light to shield, surround the vehicle with it. See it in your mind's eye."

"Black, I can't." The inside of the room was ablaze with the light from their souls. "I'm so close. Please, Black. Ah, please."

No more mister nice bear. "Don't even think about coming until I tell you to."

"Oh, god." She shivered, and her legs shook.

"Look at me, Kady. Do this for me, harness your lust, your pleasure. You did it before, I'm just asking you to be aware of where it is. Surround the vehicle so we can disappear into the dusk, but don't let your light overflow."

Sweat beaded on her lip and across her brow. Black didn't stop pleasuring her for a second. He leaned in and scraped his teeth across her neck, exactly where he wanted to bite and mark her. Could she feel how close he was to completing their mating?

Something in her changed, calmed. Slowly the light turned into a silvery translucence and the furniture around them dissolved away.

"That's it. Just a little more and I'll let you come."

The floor beneath them went next and it appeared as if they were flying over the road. The walls and the part of the vehicle where the gnomes drove were still visible. "More, *mah wah*, more."

Black had been gripping her hip with the hand not between her legs, but that wasn't using it to his advantage. He slid it around and kneaded the flesh of her plump ass. Would she like a taste of the darker pleasures he could give her?

Testing her limits, he ran a finger between the globes of her ass and stroked over her tight little hole there.

Kady whimpered but kept her calm. She thrust her hips, riding his fingers all on her own.

"Take your pleasure but control the power it brings." He swirled his finger around her anus, testing and teasing the sensitive skin.

In a blink, not only the were the walls gone, but so was the entire vehicle and the Gundersons. The only thing around them was the road, the mountains, and the late afternoon sky, all flying past.

"Keep that up and I'll give you all of the dark pleasure you can take."

Kady threw her head back, reveling in what Black could give her and her own power. "Yes, I want that. I want everything from you."

High above them in the sky two dots of shadowy light kept pace with each of their turns. Kady was in control, but her light, in this form, pure soul, attracted the spectrals like insects to a flame.

Two more appeared behind them, and still another two on either side. Had they been there all along and Kady's light made them visible, or was she attracting more?

None of them attacked or even approached. They had learned the lesson that was the burn of Kady's power.

"*Mah wah*, are you ready to explode again?"

She panted and smiled. "In more ways than one."

"Then let it all go, blow those damn spectrals away and come for me." Black pushed Kady over the edge, sliding just the tip of his finger inside her tight pucker.

She cried out, her body bucking against him. "Black, oh god, yes. Black."

Kady grabbed onto his arms, tipped her chin and stared directly into his eyes, into his heart.

Black felt his own soul swept up with hers. Together, they pulsed, building, reaching, until finally together they exploded. They were everywhere and nowhere. They were one, and a million pieces.

The spectrals around them shrieked burning as they dissolved into the white purity of the magic he and Kady made together.

Kady cried out, in pleasure or in pain, Black wasn't sure. The singe of the spectrals touching the soul magic bit under his skin.

With an imploding whoosh, they were back in their bodies, panting, melting into each other's arms. Black dropped to his knees, not being able to do anything but hold Kady's body.

"Holy ravioli. I think that's what they call mind-blowing sex." Kady breathed hard and dropped to the floor with him.

She kissed his face, his cheeks, his lips. He wanted to kiss her back, but he wasn't sure he could even move yet. Had she endured that level of pleasure and pain each time she sent her power on the attack?

"Are you okay, Black?" She nuzzled into him. "I don't know whether to say wow, thanks, or sorry. Next time we do that, you're getting off too. No more of this making it all about my orgasms."

Finally, he found the little bit of his brain that was still intact. "I'm fine. Are you in pain? I didn't know it hurt you to use your power against the spectrals."

"It didn't hurt this time as much as before. More like that tingle you get when your hands or feet have fallen asleep. The orgasm more than made up for it." She giggled.

There was always a cost to magic, on his world anyway, but knowing it didn't hurt her relieved him. "That was way beyond an orgasm, my love. I don't know what that was, but don't for a second think that I didn't get off on it."

She laughed and stroked her hand up and down his chest. "I've never made a guy come in his pants before."

"In my pants doesn't quite cover it. I think I came all over the whole damn universe."

The walls shimmered around them, slowly coming back into sight. "Damn. I thought I could hold onto the magic longer than that."

"Don't worry, my dirty curvy witch. As soon as I can once again distinguish my head from my ass, I plan to make love to you for at least twenty of the next thirty hours and I expect no less than two or three orgasms each hour. This was only round one in your training."

"You've got a thing for number of orgasms. There is no way I'm coming forty times. It's not physically possible. I'll die."

"By the time we get to New York, you'll be very well practiced at using your magic."

And they would both be exhausted and well beyond satisfied.

Over the next few hours, Kady did indeed get a better handle on her magic. They found that after about four or five more orgasms she needed only to touch Black to be able to bring up both her shield and to blow away any sneaking spectrals.

That fact gave him the perfect reason to be sure he was always at her side during the battle he knew was upcoming.

Because while she had learned to use her powers, they had their limits. Each time she shattered a spectral it reformed and returned, eventually. She could impair them, but not kill them.

Only Black understood how to destroy them forever, as he had done back in the gnomes' garden.

He hoped against the Fates that together, with the wolves, their magical mates, and the Elite team they would be able to find another solution.

The sun rose over a flat stretch of the land with fields of grain as far as the eye could see. Black had felt at home in the mountain wooded area where Kady lived. This landscape, while beautiful, felt dull to him. Or maybe it was the dread of the battle to come.

The road trip continued unencumbered and before he was ready, the gnomes drove the vehicle to a deserted parking lot, past a sign that read "trail head" and onto an unpaved road. A few minutes later they pulled up to a group of people gathered, including Titian, the fox, and the Wolf Tzar, Niko.

"Kady, do you think you can clothe us before we meet with my team and the others?"

"If I have to." She wriggled her nose and Black found himself covered.

He wore a cream-colored shirt, a black vest, blue pants

with a red stripe down the side, tall black leather boots, and some sort of weapons belt. Too bad there was no weapon.

"How's that? It's what one of my favorite spaceship captains wears."

"It will do fine. Thank you."

She gave herself similar pants in light blue and boots, with a button down tan shirt and vest. She too had a weapons belt.

He tugged her to him by her belt and ran his hands along her hips, wanting to be near her for a moment longer, knowing the hardships that lie ahead of them. "What are the belts for? We do not have weapons, except for your magic."

"Oh, I don't know, that's just what they wore in the movie"

He didn't have time to romance her any longer than that one moment because they pulled up and she dropped the shield. Right before the walls reappeared he saw the astonishment on many people in the group's faces.

The two of them climbed out of the container and were met by Titian and Niko, weapons held aloft. He held his hands up, but before they could exchange a greeting someone called out to Kady.

"Kaden Ayininkizi. I wondered when you'd finally show up." A slightly older woman, with a distinct blue sparkle in her eye came right up to Kady and hugged like they were old friends.

Ayininkizi? That was interesting.

Kady's eyebrows went up, but she returned the greeting. Black was sure Kady had never seen the older woman before in her life.

"How do you know my name?" Kady asked.

The woman patted Kady on the arm. "I have my ways."

The Gundersons climbed down out of their vehicle and were greeted by the women in the group too.

Funny that Black had fallen so far in love with his mate and hadn't even known her full given name. He stilled for a moment.

Yes, love.

The urge to claim his mate and bond the two of them together had been overwhelming from the beginning, but, until this very moment, he hadn't realized the depth of his feelings past the mating.

He loved this woman so far beyond what the Fates had decreed. Claiming, mating, sex, as explosive as it was, none of them matched the flame burning in his soul for his beautiful, sexy, smart, sensual, curvy woman.

He wanted to shout it out for everyone to know. He wanted to whisper it in her ear, for only her to hear.

After greetings were exchanged between the group and the gnomes, the other woman with the older lady extended her hand to Kady. "Hi, I'm Zara, and this is Selena. Welcome to Rogue."

Kady glanced at Black, and he shrugged, still struggling to hold his feelings in. Now was neither the time, nor the place. But soon, and for their rest of their lives, Kady would know that he loved her with everything in his being.

"Thanks? Did you know I was coming?"

Selena laughed. "Some little wolfies told me you were coming. I've been waiting on you for a while, child. I hoped you'd eventually find your way to Rogue."

"Don't mind Selena." Zara grinned in the woman's direction. "Her gift of having a super secret sneaky spy network, a little premonition about mates, and her penchant for matchmaking can seem a little intrusive at first, but you'll get used to her soon enough."

Kady didn't look convinced, but Black was glad there were other mates here to help her with understanding more about her magic and powers than he could.

Titian stepped up and extended his hand to Kady. "Sorry you had to get stuck with such a sorry excuse for a Star Marine, miss."

Black would take offense, but instead he felt the tiniest stab of jealousy when Titian winked at Kady. His bear didn't like the teasing flirtation much either and he couldn't help the low growl that rumbled up.

The whole group stared at Black, and all were completely humored. Selena even laughed and shook her head.

Titian raised his hand, never actually touching Kady. Good.

One more member of the party introduced himself. "I will refrain from shaking your hand, pretty lady, but will introduce myself. I am Doc, and Selena and I belong to each other as you belong to the bear."

Was it so obvious to everyone there that he and Kady were mates?

Titian tapped his communicator and stepped into the group. "I hate to break up your slumber party, ladies, but we've got incoming."

14

SOUL MAGIC

Crapballs. They'd only arrived and Kady had dampened her magic as much as she could to be able to give Black time to fill in his team on what they'd learned about the spectral warriors.

Plus, she'd wanted to ask Zara and Selena about a million questions about magic, including if they had to get down and dirty to access their powers too.

"Russet and Dun report that a squad of fifty human troops with – what the fuck - Spectral Warriors attached to them are headed inbound to our location. ETA less than one Earth hour." The guy from Black's team, who was too good looking for his own good, tapped on some sort of communication device. "You'd better fill us in on what you know, boss, and fast."

"Yeah, like what's a Spectral Warrior?" Zara said.

Black nodded and became the soldier Kady had seen before. Calculating and ready for a fight. "Spectral Warriors are a hybrid of soldier, weapon, and souls stolen from beings all over the galaxy."

Even the Wolf Tzar's Niko's eyes went wide at that description.

"They hide in the parts of the light spectrum most beings can't see without specialized equipment, and attack without impunity. Their mission, as far as we know, is to steal the soul of anyone they encounter."

"Steal their souls? That sounds mighty bad." Selena shook her head.

"It is worse than death. A husk of the person is left, still alive, but unable to communicate, function beyond basic daily routines, and only if they are monitored and told or shown what to do. Basically, undead."

Doc whistled, expressing with only a sound, how horrified they all were.

"My team, minus mine that were lost in the crash, has high-tech visors that has helped us them see them." He indicated to goggles Titian had dangling around his neck.

"What's your plan to defend ourselves if we can't see them coming?" Niko asked.

Black glanced at Kady and nodded. "We can see them, thanks to Kady. There is something about her powers that make the spectrals visible to the naked eye, but it also attracts them."

Niko did not look impressed by that bit of news.

"The Gundersons' wards were a temporary wall, but they can be shattered under a concentrated attack."

Titian threw his hands up in the air. "Why the fuck didn't Electra send us some gnomes when this whole shit storm started? I'd sure as shit liked to have known about magical wards."

Black wondered the same thing. Late in the night, between bouts of love making, he'd confided in Kady. He didn't understand why his superior, Electra, had waited until news that the spectrals were gathering on Earth to have them meet up with Niko and his town of supernatural beings.

Electra had seen what the magic bearers of Earth could do. She and another Star Marine named Cole were the few in the force that did, until Black and his team had been briefed.

Margreth spoke up giving the other witches the information Black couldn't. "It's a simple no-entry protective ward. You wolf mates can probably make stronger ones than I can.

"Yes, but how long do the wards last?" Zara asked.

Black filled her in. "Depends on how many attack and how badly they want to get in. Spectrals will sacrifice themselves to break through to get to fresh souls."

His words gave Zara a visible shiver. "What do we do once they break through the wards?"

"Kady has also learned to injure them, more or less, but it's temporary."

Zara frowned. "Is it a spell? We can replicate that."

All eyes turned on her. Uh-oh. A few days ago, she was just a chubby geek girl hiding out in her tiny house in the woods. Hold up though, she'd come a long way since then. She had some badass powers that could do amazing things. She pushed her glasses up her nose deciding it was time to get her butt in the game.

"I don't really understand what it is. I'm new to the

whole magic thing. I was hoping you could help me understand it better."

Selena touched her arm. "Show us, Kady girl. We'll figure it out from there."

Kady glanced over at Black, who had a lusty look on his face. Thank goodness, they'd worked on this, so they didn't have to make-out or get naked to get this part of her magic revved up anymore. Kady reached out and took Black's hand. "See, uh, the first time we realized it was my magic that made them visible, we were…"

Black had a big ole shiteatin' grin on his face. Just like a dude to be all proud that his dick had made the magic.

Swirls of light rose from her skin and drifted between the two of them.

Selena and Zara exchanged glances, seeming to confirm something with each other.

"Then when we escaped the attack from the TFO and on the trip down here, I used my power both as the shield you saw and kind of like a bomb going off." Kady continued to push the power she'd learned to harness out, first surrounding her and Black until they were inside her shield and they disappeared from the rest of the group's view.

"Nice stealth, boss. You wanna let us in on that?"

Kady pushed the shield out further until it encompassed everyone. "I've only been able to do the explosion part when, well, ahem…" Kady could feel the heat bubbling under her skin like she'd had too many glasses of red wine.

Black continued for her. "I kissed, wait, what did you call it, *mah wah*? Ah, I remember. I kissed the bejeesus out of her and was getting into her pants to make her come."

Kady turned purple. She had to remember to council Black on his use of earth vernacular, and about the privacy of their sex lives.

Selena nodded. "I see. I know where Kady's magic comes from now."

The rest of the group looked at her, waiting. This Selena had a flair for the dramatic and waited another minute before she let the rest of them in on the knowledge. "It's Soul Magic."

Zara nodded, confirming what Selena said. "Few mates have access to its powers, notably those with shifter lineage. It has something to do with how and why you can shift between forms."

Black tilted his head to the side. "Yes, when I was trying to help Kady use her power I explained it to her in the same way the shift was taught to me as a cub."

Zara tapped her lips, thinking. "I don't think we have any other bear decedents in town, though."

"But we do have soul mates." Selena took Doc's hand. "We may be able to use that to our advantage."

"Can you show us the explosion?" Zara's mate asked.

Kady nodded. She closed her eyes, trying to pull up the feelings, the passion Black brought out in her. Something glimmered to the surface, but it was weak compared to before. Black squeezed her hand and rubbed his thumb across her wrist.

She tried again, and a small whoosh blew past the group. They all got a glazed over, I-need-a-cigarette look on their faces.

Niko was the first to recover. He pulled Zara into his

arms and nuzzled her. Then he addressed Kady. "Interesting. There's something in your magic I recognize. It's very cold."

Zara cuddled into Niko's arms. "Don't say that, Niko. I kind of liked it. Besides, she's putting her heart and literally her soul into this."

Niko kissed Zara on the top of the head. "I don't mean she is unfeeling. There was a hell of a lot of emotion in that spell. I can feel the telltale power of the Moon in her magic. Whatever she's yielding is as old as time. I don't entirely understand it, but I think we can use it to our advantage when you call upon our souls for the same spell, my love."

"I like it. Phooey on those spectrals, I'll take that spell home and use it all night long." Selena declared.

"Selena." Zara used a chastising tone.

"What?"

Titian dropped to one knee and pulled a weapon from his boot. "You all can have fun with your sex spells later. Spectrals dead ahead."

"We need to get into the Reserve." Niko pointed to the trailhead behind them. "There are defensible locations, caves. I suggest we pair off and work at the spells to hide and push them back. Gundersons you come with us."

"Niko, wait. It won't do us any good to hold them at bay. We could be doing that forever." Zara tugged at Niko's arm.

"She's right. There is one more thing I hadn't gotten to yet." Black's voice had gone deep and dark.

The sound of it sent a chill through Kady that she hadn't expected. For the first time, she saw the toll being a warrior had taken on him. Lines around his mouth and eyes she hadn't seen before.

"There is a way to kill the spectrals."

Titian rolled his eyes like he'd known Black was keeping something back. "Fuck, yeah. We've scoured the universe for that kind of intel. Why didn't you tell us in the first place, boss?"

Muscles worked in Black's jaw as if he were trying to hold in the words that could mean their safety. "Kill the body of the stolen soul."

Titian lost his excitement and some of his color. "Fuck me," he whispered.

Oh no. Black's mother's soul had been stolen. How many more family members had these brave warriors lost? How many might be lost today?

If he or any of them had to kill a loved one to fight these horrible monsters, the spectrals wouldn't have any souls left to steal, because they would all be lost.

Kady hadn't called upon the Universe to help her since she'd become more acquainted with her magic, but she did now.

Dear sweet Universe. Thank you for bringing Black into my life and helping me realize the power within me. Please help me keep him safe and help him find a way to defeat the enemy without losing his own soul.

Kady's magic rose to the surface, swirling around her in a dance of light. Screeches wrenched through the air above them. She looked up into the sky and saw the forms of dozens of spectral warriors swarming like killer bees.

May all their souls be saved.

15

BRING IT ON

"Incoming." Titian called out and pointed toward the sky. The shadowy slippery figures of a dozen spectral warriors bore down on them. "Go, go, go. Into the forest."

Black grabbed Kady's hand. "Can you push them back to give us time to get into defensible positions?"

She nodded. His fierce curvy warrior.

Their hands glowed where they touched, and she drew the power, closed her eyes and pushed it out in a burst of light toward the spectrals.

Unlike all the other times Kady had used her magic the spectrals had dissipated before their eyes. Some had reformed but were visibly weakened. This time, when she threw her burst of power at them, they swerved, bobbed, and weaved around the lights.

"They've learned." Black shouted. He was surprised it had taken them this long. "We need to find a defensible position, where the mates can work together."

A tide of soldiers, blank faced, but in battle gear,

marching forward, weapons drawn, appeared on the dirt road.

Doc shouted, "We won't make it without some help. Where's a tank when you need one?"

They heard an engine rev behind them and the screech of tires coming up fast. Black glanced over his shoulder and saw Kady's red and white vehicle break free from the restraints of the trailer it was tied down to and accelerate into the parking lot.

It took out three soldiers, knocking them to the ground and running right over them before racing across the road and pulling up in front of their group.

"Herbie?" Kady's jaw dropped at the sight of her vehicle, engine running, ready to go.

It honked its horn for her.

"Well, hello, Herbie. Long time, no see." Selena patted the side of the vehicle and jumped into the open bed of the back. "Come on, people. Don't stand there, we've got a fight on our hands."

Black pulled Kady into the cockpit while the others piled into the back. "He is yours, drive him into the forest, see if you can find a covered position."

She threw the vehicle's gear control forward and grabbed the steering wheel. Her small spiky pet sat atop it.

"I'd be surprised you're here, Percy, but I'm clean out of surprise. Nice to see you, little buddy."

They sped down the road, but instead of following it, Kady steered them over the edge of a stream.

"Hold on to your butts." The Herbie accelerated and by the feel of it, hovered over the ground. They flew over rocks, past trees and into the shadows and cover of the dense trees.

Black pointed to a huge tree with what looked like an entrance into the freaking underworld at its base. "There, quickly."

Kady nodded and aimed them for the hole in the tree. "It's too tight. We're not going to fit."

She wrinkled and wiggled her nose. Just as they were about to hit the tree, the Herbie transformed beneath them, tumbling all but Kady into a cave filled with dirt and tree roots.

Kady came to a soft landing sitting astride a broom. "Sorry. I was going for a big broom for everyone to ride on."

Black would contemplate that bit of sorcery later. "Zara, Selena, quickly, erect Margreth's wards around the cave."

The women, joined by Margreth, said a series of words, and drew symbols in the air. In a breath, a buzz and a short flash burst around them. Not a second too soon. The first wave of spectrals crashed into the protection the wards offered.

"With this many spectral warriors attacking, we don't have much time before they break through the wards." Margreth pointed to several spots that were already showing cracks.

"My magic didn't work on them this time. We're stuck in here." Kady walked back and forth in the small space afforded by the cave, holding her broom and biting her lip.

Black took her free hand to stop her nervous pacing. "They've learned our attack strategy. So, we'll have to change it up."

Titian looked out the front of the cave and waved the rest of them over to see. "Look, the troops are gathering in expected areas. The way I see it, the best chance we have is to eliminate the soldiers and the spectrals attached to them."

Which meant killing humans who were likely innocent. Black knew he, Titian, and Niko had taken lives before in the line of duty, but not innocents.

"Suggestions?" Titian was a crafty strategist, so if anyone could come up with a plan to get them out of this FUBAR, the fox could.

"If the witches can spread their magic like a directed scatter bomb, we could follow with our side arms to eliminate the humans."

Niko nodded. "I don't carry anymore, but I still have the power of the Moon. I'll rip out the bastards throats."

"Doc, what have you got?" Titian asked.

"A few tricks up my sleeve, young pup."

Black folded his arms and stared at each of the member of his impromptu team. "Good, then let's make some magic. Kady, show 'em how it's done."

Kady reached out, touching his arm and drew on the heat between them. "It comes from deep inside, and I have to pull on the magic first, and then transform it into the shield. When it comes into contact with the spectrals they literally dissolve. I have to warn you, it hurts, especially the first time."

She let her magic recede and stepped across the space to take Zara and Selena's hands. "I don't know how else to show you, but to bring it up in the same way I do with Black."

Kady closed her eyes and took a deep breath. Before she

blew it out again her soft glow had encompassed both women.

"Oh, yeah. I got it," Selena said.

Zara laughed. "It's a bit like foreplay."

Zara and Selena both took the hands of their mates. Zara closed her eyes and soon a soft amber light glowed on her skin. Selena's magic was a mix of blue and silver.

Black put his arms around Kady's waist. Her golden light grew and overwhelmed the room. "Niko, Doc, it will help to strengthen the magic if you can, uh, show some affection to your ladies."

"Lay one on me, Doc baby." Selena pulled her mate down for a kiss.

Zara took Niko's hand and placed it over her belly. Her own light grew almost exponentially and matched Kady's. If he had to guess, Black would say she was pulling on the power of three souls, not just the two.

"Do you feel how it's surrounding you? Try changing its direction, pushing it out. That's how I turn it into the shield, and a weapon."

The other people in the room dissolved from view as Kady surrounded them in her magic.

"I think I've got it, but you two are the only ones who disappeared." Zara's voice penetrated the shimmering translucence.

Kady lowered her shield and the rest of the people reappeared. "I'm sorry. I don't know how else to help. I wish I knew more about how magic works."

Selena tilted her head to the side, thinking. "I've been around magic a lot of years, and what I do know is everyone's gifts are a bit different. We've got the basics of your spell, but I doubt either Zara or I will get that disappearing part down. We can still fight the spooks off."

"Once they break the wards, there's no putting the same ones up or even reinforcing them. I suggest you all get ready, because here they come." Margreth pointed to the mouth of the cave where three spectrals were all flying at a crack together."

"Fates be on our side." Black brought the bear as close to the surface as he could without shifting and stepped in front of Kady. He saw Titian do the same with his fox and stand in front of the Gundersons.

"On my mark, ladies, let it loose."

The spectrals crashed the wards, one recoiling back, but the other two bursting through the barrier. Their soldiers followed fast behind.

"Now, now, now."

Black shifted fully into the bear and let out a great roar shaking the cave and throwing the soldiers on their asses.

The full power of the soul magic whooshed past him. One spectral swerved to avoid Kady's light but got caught by Selena's.

Zara's magic obliterated the other spectral at the same time as Niko shifted and ripped the soldier's head from his body.

Black stepped forward gaining ground with each burst of magic and light from behind him. He slashed and tore at the chests and limbs of the soldiers nearest to them. A team of three jumped out from behind a boulder and fired their weapons.

This time he was prepared for the sting of the metal projectiles. He rose up to his full bear height and bore the fire, protecting his team behind him.

Titian fired his weapon, taking all three out just as their spectrals were swooping down on Black's head.

The Gundersons helped even without conventional weapons. Turned out Sigar had a mean fallenball arm, tossing rocks the size of his head at the soldiers. Margreth erected quick temporary wards, blocking the spectrals paths.

The group tore through two dozen soldiers and their spectrals with their combination of might, fight, and magic. Black suppressed all emotion, only allowing the warrior bear's instincts to guide him in keeping Kady and the others safe and pressing forward.

"Black, dead ahead," Titian shouted, "check out the asshole wearing the black suit and sunglasses."

"That's not an asshole," Kady cut in, "that's a douchecanoe."

Titian snorted. "Whatever he is, he's the head of this Fates-forsaken hydra. We take him out, the rest will fall easily."

Black found the target Titian and Kady identified. Tree weasel. A dark hollowness filled his chest. It wasn't fear, at least not for himself. Something compelled him to do everything he could to get closer and attack the TFO man who they'd crossed paths with too many times now.

A growl grew from the deepest part of his chest. Swirling above was a spectral, that was not any part of the tree weasel man's soul but was his mother's.

A hatred Black had never known before stretched across

his muscles and tore at his heart. He didn't know how, but this lowly, puny, worthless human man had stolen his mother's soul and now had control of it.

He would kill the bastard.

A new rain of weapons' fire barreled down on them, striking him in the neck, the chest, his shoulders. His fur became coated with blood, his power to heal not keeping up with the new wounds. Still he pressed forward, knowing Kady had his back.

Her magic slashed out, no longer a shield, but a sword, a saber of light. The spectrals weren't fast enough to avoid her strikes. The soldiers weren't cognizant enough to escape his claws.

They were close enough now to see the sweat pooling on the face of the tree weasel. He was scared, and he should be, his death was impending, and it would not be quick or painless.

They had taken out all the other soldiers and spectrals except for the final ten troops surrounding the lone man.

Black would love to charge forward and sever the jugular with his teeth, but he couldn't leave Kady or the team exposed. One step, two. Closer they crept, Black no longer feeling any pain from the weapons shooting at him.

Tree weasel raised a communicator to his face. Calling for back up now was futile. This day's battle was nearly over. Victory would be Black's soon.

A bladed ship dropped down into the canopy of the forest, its blades narrowly missing the tree tops. Fuck, if they dropped a ladder as they had before, he would miss this opportunity to avenge his mother.

Black shifted back into a man and pulled Kady to him. "Lend me your power, imbue me with the strength to take out our enemy."

Kady stretched up on her tiptoes and pressed a kiss to his lips. It tingled and burned the same as the very first time he'd touched her. Her magic flowed over him, into him, filling his heart and soul, until he was sure he would burst. He broke their kiss and roared into the sky.

"I love you, Black," she whispered and stepped back, stumbling. Doc caught her before she could fall.

She was pale and exhausted. He moved to help her, be there for her, but she held up a hand and waved him off. "Go. Save the world, *mah wah*."

Her words filled him with even more power. He looked to Niko. "Take care of her."

Doc's nod was all he needed. "Titian, give me cover."

"Fuck, yeah. Zara, Selena, hit those bastards with everything you've got left, ladies." Titian filled the air with suppressing fire, and whips of blue, amber, and silver light snapped through the air.

Black put his head down and ran forward at full speed. The bladed ship was dropping fast, and the bastard was already moving toward it. Only a few more steps and he could tear the limbs from the man.

The spectral that was his mother's soul hovered, unmoving, until the tree weasel raised his arm and let a glowing amulet drop and dangle.

Black's soul ember. The piece of his soul intended for his mate, for Kady.

Bile rose at the back of his throat, filling his mouth with

pure bitterness. No wonder the spectrals and the TFO had been able to track them down again and again. It wasn't just Kady's powers that attracted them. They literally had a piece of his soul.

The bastard pointed the ember at Black and the spectral screeched, rushing at him. He heard the shouts behind him for Zara and Selena to shoot the spectral down, but their attempts missed.

If he could get to the ember before the spectral attacked, at least there would be a part of him for Kady to have. A part of his soul to soothe hers when he was gone.

A meter before Black reached the bastard, the spectral flew over his shoulder, skimming his skin with its cold touch.

Spectral warriors didn't miss, they attacked their victims mercilessly. If his soul was not already ripped from his body, he was not the prey.

A chasm of fear opened in his chest. If not him, then...

He pivoted mid-stride and watched in utter horror as the spectral tore through the air, directly for Kady.

"Nooooo." The light of his life could not be stolen. He transformed instantly into the bear and bounded forward, overtaking the speed of the spectral in a moment.

It screeched one last time and dove for Kady. Black pushed off the ground, his back legs filled with the power of a thousand bears, throwing himself into the air, blocking the spectral warrior's path.

For Kady.

In an instant light flashed before his eyes and a pain worse than a thousand cuts lashed through him. His soul was torn from his body and all the hatred and darkness of every being for a thousand millennia overtook him.

He tried to reach out, call to Kady, to tell her how he loved her. In a final fiery blast, his thoughts and free will splintered, his mind, body, and soul shattered.

16

DARK WARRIOR

"Black!" Kady screamed, pain tearing through her so deep she lost her next breath.

Black's body dropped to the ground, shimmering back into the form of a man. He lay unmoving in the dirt.

The helicopter swooped down, snatching up the TFO man. Titian fired his weapon, striking the metal. The copter wobbled but continued its flight path and within second flew out of reach and across the sky.

The spectral warrior that had been Black's mother, that had stolen Black's soul, drifted into the air following the path of the chopper.

Titian fired again, but the helicopter was out of range. He raised a communicator to his mouth and shouted to his team to intercept the escaping agent.

Kady rushed to Black's side and dropped to the ground, throwing her arms around him. His chest moved up and down, she could feel his pulse in her tight grip on him, but there was no light in his eyes, no spark of his soul connecting with hers.

Where was Black's soul, or the spectral warrior it had become? She blinked, holding back the tears, and his form appeared, hovering above her, pulsing as its shape grew, a mass of unformed liquid shadow.

"No no no no no no no. Black, you come back to me right now. You cannot do this. You cannot leave me alone."

She raised her voice to the sky, seeking to connect with the stolen soul. It shimmered, growing less translucent and more shadowy by the second.

"Black," she shouted at the spectral forming before her eyes, "don't do this. You are mine and I am yours. Please, Black, please come back."

Kady pulled his slack body into her arms and rocked his form, crying out his name, pleading with the shadow to return over and over.

She'd been abandoned by everyone who should have been important in her life, wounded and scarred by the missing connections, stolen from her before she could even remember. She'd survived on her own, building a lonely independence around herself. She hadn't thrived. Not until Black.

"Please, Universe. Please don't take him from me now."

The new spectral warrior screeched like a hurt animal lashing out. Deep in her own broken soul, Kady knew he was in terrible pain. She tried to call up her magic, wrap it around him, soothe him in her light. If only she could reach him, maybe she could pull him back from the abyss forming between them.

All she could manage was a warm glow across her skin, that she wrapped gently around Black's body.

The new spectral screeched again, louder this time, and dove toward her.

"Kady, look out." Zara shot a steady stream of magic at the spectral warrior.

"No, stop!" Kady raised her hand, pulling from the depths of her being to call up the magic that had been there only moments before.

Her hand glowed a deep gold, but the magic wouldn't go, it wouldn't do her bidding. She wanted, needed to block Zara's amber defense and protect Black's soul.

Without his light mixing with hers, adding to her power, she had nothing. Her heart sank through the emptiness inside of her leaving, only a sad, angry desperation in its wake.

The spectral warrior weaved around Zara's magic, bearing down on Kady. Selena added her blue and silver light to the battle, deflecting the spectral a fraction of a second before it could hit.

It recoiled, and dove at her, two, three, four times. Zara and Selena formed a shield over the top and around her. Margreth reinforced the shield with a new ward.

Still, the spectral beat down, frantic to get to her.

"Black." Kady reached up, holding his body in one arm, grasping for his soul with her other.

She could see the form of his face in shadow, beautiful, but angry, so angry. He clawed at the magic around her.

He wanted her soul. He wouldn't have to steal it, she'd readily give it to him. She already had. What if she stood up, pushed through the barriers between them, let him take her?

A calm settled over her, extinguishing the last bit of light inside her. What was the light without Black, anyway?

She lay his head and shoulders down, touched her fingers to her lips, and then to his. Standing forced the shields around her to expand. They fluctuated and thinned. As if Black's spectral understood her intentions, it doubled its efforts to get to her, shattering the ward.

Kady pushed her fingertips through the open edges of the ward, touching Zara and Selena's magic.

They yelled, but their voices were muted, filtered through a thick layer of grief. Didn't matter what they said, anyway. Kady pushed through the swirls of blue, amber, and silver light.

Take me, Black. Take me with you.

The spectral Black grabbed her hand, burning her from the inside out. The pain ripped through her, weakening her until her knees gave out. Her body dangled in the air, held aloft by the grip Black's dark soul had on her.

Her thoughts fell away, leaving a misshapen anger behind. She wanted to scream, but her lungs had seized.

"Kaden." A strong voice yelled out, reaching through the blackness and she was hit from the side. Her body hurtled through the air, being snatched, torn away from the grasp of the spectral.

She crashed into the ground, her glasses falling into the dirt by her head, her eyes flooded with bright New York sunlight.

The air whooshed back into her lungs and a cool light soothed the injuries to her hand and soul.

"Kaden, m'lady, are you all right?"

A man, a buck-naked one, was sprawled out on top of her, running his hands over her arms, face, and hands.

"Get off me."

Niko and Doc grabbed the man by his shoulders and yanked him to his feet. But Zara and Selena didn't move to help at all.

Kady rolled away, grabbing her glasses in the process and shoved them on her face. Who was this naked man, and why had he tried to stop her from giving up her soul?

She looked him up and down, avoiding his package as best she could. He had spiky hair, a short stubby nose, and brown eyes she recognized.

"I'm not a threat," he said to the men holding him, "Kaden is my mistress. I was only trying to save her."

Doc looked to Selena who nodded. They released him, and he reached his hand down, in offer to help Kady to her feet.

She shook her head and he sat on the ground beside her. "Don't cry, sweet Kaden. You can rub my belly if it will make you feel better."

Rub his belly? The only belly she'd ever rubbed while crying was...

"Percy?"

"At your service, m'lady." Percy winked and dipped his head in a bow.

She looked at her hands but didn't feel the magic there. She couldn't have done this. Both Zara and Selena shook their heads when she asked them with a glance.

"But you're a hedgehog."

"When you needed me to be your companion. I am your

familiar, I am whatever you need me to be. Now you need a Spock to your Kirk, a Chewie to your Han, an R2 to your D2."

He spoke passionately and raised a knife into the air. It looked like the knife-like weapon Agent Douchecanoe had pulled on her.

"Be careful with that." He might look like a muscled, well-endowed naked man, but he'd been a pet up until a minute ago.

"I was kind of hoping it was a light-saber." He lifted the knife over their heads and pushed a button, but nothing happened. He sighed and let the knife fall to the ground. "I always wanted to be a Jedi, ever since the first time you played the Star Wars movies for me and fed me popcorn."

Kady wrapped her arms around herself. "That's funny. I always wished I were a Jedi too. But now I have powers just as badass as the Force, and they didn't do me a damn bit of good."

"But m'lady, what do you mean? This is the moment you've been waiting for your entire life. You have to rescue your Han from the evil clutches of Jabba."

She shook her head. The tears she'd held back earlier pooled at the edges of her eyes. "The only way to save Black is to free his soul by killing his body. I can't do that."

Percy tsked. "Now is no time to let your fear turn you to the Dark side. Look where that got Anni and Amidala."

She turned away from Percy. She wanted only to hide from the world again. "Get your head out of your butt. This isn't a movie."

Percy stood, towering over her. He pointed and shook his

finger at her. "No, you get your head out of your butt. You are a witch, descendent of a powerful line of Romani witches. They died defending you and your sisters, so that you might live and fulfill your destiny. You are a warrior. Be one now."

She shook her head, ignoring his words. It was probably a story he'd seen in a movie anyway. Sounded like one. "I'm no warrior."

Selena came over, patted Percy on the butt and joined her on the ground. "Your name, Kaden, means warrior. It is who you are. There's power in names, so whether you believe it or not, you are a warrior."

She didn't feel like she could fight anything. "A name a family I've never even met gave me. It has no meaning, and I certainly don't have any power, with or without it."

Zara joined them, making them into a small circle of women. "You have more power than you know. I didn't put it together when Selena said your name, when we met, but now I know who you are. When I became the Tsarina I had to do a lot of study of supernatural history. You come from a long line of witches, your mother was a witch."

Kady shook her head. "Did you know my mother? Because, I didn't, and she didn't give me anything but an abandonment complex."

"No. Your heritage is very clear now that Percy has revealed it. You're clearly from the legend of the Ayinin sisters. You've been lost to the world, until now."

Wait. What? Percy's story was real?

"Percy? My family died? I have sisters?"

He scoffed. "Of course, you do."

"Was my father a witch too? I guess, does that make him a wizard, a warlock?"

Kady's brain was fried. She couldn't focus, couldn't get her mind around this story about her family, not that and the loss of Black.

Selena shook her head. "Your father was a bear."

Percy interjected. "You're the offspring, the first daughter of the Warrior Anatolian Bears."

"The Romani witches have intermingled with shifters back before the dark ages when shifters were hunted." Selena was going to have to share where she learned all of this with Kady someday.

Selena nodded. "That's got to be where you get your easy use of Soul Magic, and of course, your name. *Ayinin kizi*, bear's daughter."

Bear's daughter. Was that what had attracted Black to her in the first place?

"Does that mean there are bear people who aren't aliens?"

"Of course. We don't see many in Rogue. There are more in the mountains. But we can probably help you find some of your people, if not your family."

She didn't care about her family. They had died, abandoning her long ago. The only person who meant family to her had been Black.

"It doesn't matter. I have no power without Black by my side."

Percy pushed his way into the witches' circle and sat on Kady's lap. They were going to have to talk about how he wasn't hedgehog sized anymore. "Even if you weren't a witch, you're still the only person who can save Black's soul. His is crying out for you. Go to him, bring him back."

She pushed Percy off, then stood and backed away from them all. Too much had happened to her in too short a time to take anymore.

"I can't," she screamed, all her sadness, frustration, and fear pouring out with her tears.

Percy followed her, prodding her in the chest with his hand. "Kaden Ayininkizi, I was created to be your companion, your familiar and stand with you in times of strife. I watched and waited for you to realize your powers and did a god-damned happy dance when that crazy alien bear showed up in your life."

She backed away from him, frantic to find an escape, to get away, hide from the world, from the magic, from the grief.

Percy didn't relent. "Don't think for one magical minute I am going to stand idly by poking you with my spines while you wallow around crying for the soul only you can save."

"Percy. Dammit. I can't save him. He's gone, my magic is gone. It doesn't matter where I came from or what any of you thought I could do. Don't you understand? I am back to being nothing."

"Nothing?" Percy's voice boomed, echoing off the rock walls. "You wield the strongest magic of all. The Universe bows to your will. The power was always there, your soulmate awakened it. You were born to be a warrior. Be one, dammit."

She shook her head, sucking in gasps of breath, staving back Percy's claims. "I don't even know how to use the magic without Black."

"Your souls are already intertwined. Even in his twisted state, he is still yours and you are his. All you have to do is feel it inside. He's there." Percy laid his hand over her heart.

She closed her eyes, searched inside for any trace of Black. The tears bubbled over and streaked down her face. She couldn't feel him, only her broken heart.

Percy lowered his voice and spoke from his core to hers. "You've hidden from the world, let it beat you down, told yourself the flaws were within. They aren't. Greatness is in you. Find the magic inside, Kaden. Search your heart, your soul, your very being. Become who you truly are."

Kady closed her eyes, letting the tears stream down her face. Her body shook with sobs. She cried for Black, she cried for the family she had never known, she cried for the life she had been denied.

Years of self-doubt, self-recrimination washed away in the flood of emotion. The walls she'd placed around her heart and mind cracked and tumbled, crumbling to pieces.

There were scars on the fresh new layers of Kady, and they would take time to heal. They would always be a part of her. But scars were more than a sign of a wound, they also meant healing. They meant she had survived and become stronger.

That was knowledge she could take into battle.

The only battle, the only mission that mattered to her now.

Save Black's soul, save the world.

17

FATES FORSAKEN

Her soul burned like nothing else in the universe. He needed to rip it from her body, bring it into his new world. The blaze coming from deep within her scorched him just from looking at it.

Its beauty and light ate away at the darkness and must be extinguished. Then the shadow remaining would be added to his own blackness.

The witch cried out, reached for him, giving him the opportunity he needed to shatter her.

He seized her hand, suffering the effects of the other witches' magic to get to her. Her touch burned so torturously. It fueled his anger, his need to take her.

Just as he had a hold, dragging the light from her into the darkness, a creature, who's soul didn't match its form snatched her from his grip.

No. They would all pay for this.

She must be his. She already was.

He gathered the darkness around him and prepared to

pursue. He would sacrifice anything to seize what belonged to him.

The darkness didn't obey his commands. He screamed for it, but it deserted him. A pinpoint of light beckoned through the dark despair around him and ripped him away from the witch.

He was being pulled away, dragged from his dark desire. He scratched at the air, flailing, trying to free himself from the cursed beam of illumination that had a grip on him.

It yanked, sending him rocketing further from his witch and her undamned soul.

Within a moment her light faded to a faint glow from far away and he was forced to join other dark shadows like him. They were pulled into a subterranean lair. It stank of unfettered souls.

The anger, hate, and sadness of the other warriors permeated his being. He was one with the wraiths of darkness, and they were with him.

One black soul near to him overwhelmed him with its sadness. The hate had fallen away from it, making it weak.

He recognized his maker. It was a wonder that soul had been the one to steal his own into this new world.

A human creature made sounds that drew his attention. "Well, isn't this interesting. I wondered what this bit of alien jewelry might be good for. Now, I see."

This creature stood in the center of the dark souls, making unintelligible noise. It held the light in its hand, the tiny beacon that had dragged him away from his witch. The ember of light was encased in something that he knew couldn't be permeated. He screamed his frustration.

That bit of light was his. No, it was him. It had to be darkened and destroyed.

The creature focused his energy on the ember and drew, no forced, his black shadow to his side. "This will come in very handy, I think."

This creature's light was a mere flicker compared to the soul of the witch. Barely worth stealing.

He dove for it regardless, wanting to dampen even its faded glint. A mass of dark souls blocked his path and, in an instant, he understood the creature was a means to an end. Allowing that soul to remain in his form meant a path to victory over this entire world.

Another creature entered the room, this one sparkling with both dark and light energy, glowing red. This one was to be left untouched as well. For now.

"You fool. You've lost fifty newly formed troops, putting us behind, and given the Star Marines and witches the advantage." She struck out at the male creature, knocking him to the floor.

Her hatred gathered around her, drifting through the air, delicious and enticing. "Take the soul ember and the spectral warrior and get me that witch."

The weak human creature whined. "She's powerful. You should have warned me."

"You should have captured her in Colorado before she realized her power. Get her this time, or don't bother coming back, unless you've join the ranks of the spectral warriors."

The weak-souled creature pulled him along with the draw of the ember, leaving the other warriors behind.

"I'll have to set a trap for her, cut her off from her friends before they can get back to Rogue."

He could feel the malice and greed coming off the creature in eddies. He could feed on that for the time being. The creature too coveted his witch. He would happily forfeit the benefit of keeping the creature around if it meant he could ensnare the soul of his witch.

Her soul was his, and his alone.

18

UNFORGIVEN

Kady held Black's hand, she held it tight. He looked at her, at their hands, and back. The closest to an expression she could see was maybe confusion.

She folded his fingers around her own, closing his hand. That he seemed to understand, because when she let go of his fingers, they remained gripping hers.

"I know you don't understand me right now, my love, but, I promise I'm going to do everything I can to get your soul back.

She wasn't even sure it was possible, and that hurt so hard she wanted to punch someone in the face. Someone who wore a black suit, black sunglasses and drove a douche canoe.

"Can somebody please put some clothes on Percy?" Doc held his hand out blocking his view from Percy's mid-section.

"Aw, that would be such a shame." Selena snuggle into Doc's side, teasing him. Probably.

Zara flicked her hand and put Percy into tight jeans, a sleeveless western style plaid shirt, a cowboy hat, and boots.

"Hey, Kaden, look at me, I'm Bronco Billy, no wait, the outlaw Josey Wales." Percy laughed and danced around in the dirt, grabbing Zara up and singing to her. "Throw your arms 'round this honky tonk man."

"What is he yammering about?" Niko asked.

"Hey Sara, need a couple of mules? I've got a fistful of dollars."

Kady smiled, and it didn't even crack her face. "He thinks he's Clint Eastwood. We may have watched a few old Westerns together."

"Ha ha. For a few dollars more, I'll paint your wagon."

Before Percy could come up with his next cheesy line a spaceship swooped down into the forest. It blew dust and debris everywhere as it hovered and landed.

A door on the side of the vessel slid open and two men, identical to each other with matching beards and who were each as good-looking as Black stepped from the ship.

"Stat rep." One of them said. No greeting, no nothing. These must be men in Black's team. He had mentioned he worked with his brothers.

Titian stepped up and replied. "Big ass battle against fifty some odd troops and spectrals, and one TFO man." He glanced over at Kady, then back to the men. "Black is down."

The two men looked at each other and then at Kady. "Release his body to us, woman."

Oh, hell no. Kady narrowed her eyes and reached inside to call up her magic, forgetting that she'd lost it. Something tingled low in her belly and a warm glow built up.

Huh.

Titian stepped between her and the advancing men. "Stop. She is his mate."

"Where is his soul ember? It will show us the truth of that." One of the men pushed past Titian and knelt next to Black. He pushed the collar of Black's shirt aside, examining his neck.

The other man watched. "Do you have the ember, woman?"

Kady would not be intimidated by them, their words, or their actions. She raised her chin and tightened her grip on Black's hand. "I don't know what that means."

The kneeling man reached for her, pushing the neckline of her shirt aside before she could stop him. "You are not marked, you do not wear his ember. You are not his mate. He is not yours."

This was some ripe baloney bullshit. Kady lashed out, shooting a golden beam of light from her free hand and toppling both men on their asses.

That act, calling on her magic again and having it respond felt…right.

"Don't you ever, ever say that Black is not mine. We belong to each other."

She hadn't known she was going to hit them with her magic like that. She'd only meant to push the closest man's arm away. The light had erupted from her hand and she welcomed its glow back.

She could and would defend both her mate and their relationship.

The men got back on their feet and Kady waited for their retaliation. She was ready for them.

Neither man moved, but both cracked smiles. One of them stretched his neck, rubbing it where he'd landed on it in the dirt. "You are a feisty one. Maybe you are Black's match."

"We are Black's brothers. I am Russet, and this is Dunn. If you are his mate, we are sorry for your loss." They glanced at Black who had simply sat there holding her hand through the entire altercation.

"We also lost both of our parents to the spectral warriors. Losing Black is... a blow. I promise you we will avenge him."

Kady stood and coaxed Black to his feet. She brushed a bit of dust from his cheek. "He is not lost. I'm going to get his soul back."

The brothers glanced at each other, then to Niko and his mate. "Is this possible?"

Niko shook his head. "Don't ask me. The way the magic on this planet works blows my mind every damn day. If the witch says she can get his soul back, you two better sign on to help her."

Kady wasn't sure herself she could do what she'd declared, but when she checked to see what Zara's reaction to what Niko said, Zara dipped her chin in a you-can-do-it nod.

In unison, the brothers stepped to Kady and took a knee before her.

"We are at your disposal," Russet said.

Dunn nodded. "Tell us how we can help."

"You can start by telling me what a soul ember is." Something Black had mentioned niggled in her memory. She knew this ember was important.

The guys stood and reached into their shirts. Each pulled out a pendant hanging from a cord around their necks.

They matched the two halves of an orb together, the stone sparked and glowed for a moment before fading and revealing an engraving of a bear's paw print on its center.

Dunn explained. "In our solar system, when shifters come of age and learn to harness the power of the animal inside of them, a witch harvests a sliver of our souls and encases it in an unbreakable spell."

The two dropped the amulets back beneath their shirts. Russet continued. "This ember is for our mates. The Fates decide who we will match with and when. We know we are in the presence of our chosen one when the ember burns and glows."

Ah, yes. Black had said his soul ember glowed right before they had met. She'd never seen any sort of amulet on him like what these twin brothers wore.

Wait. Yes, she had. She'd seen it in the hands of Agent Douchecanoe.

Dammit. "That TFO man has Black's ember."

Titian trotted over when she said that. "Fuck me, that's about as bad as the news that we have to kill Black."

The brothers raised their weapons. "Why would you kill the living body of our brother?"

Titian held up his hands. "Black discovered the key, and we tried and tested it." He motioned to the bodies of the soldiers littering the ground. "It's the only way to defeat the spectral. Kill the body, kill the soul."

One twin glared at Titian, while the other raised an eyebrow at Kady.

"The witch will recover his soul," Russ stated, no doubts.

Dunn completed the thought. "And reunite it with his body."

Ooh, Kady hoped her mouth wasn't writing checks her magic couldn't cash. She had to believe it was true and force away any doubts. She didn't know how, she didn't know when, but Kady would reclaim her mate.

Rawr. She is woman witch bear, hear her roar.

Russ's other eyebrow went up. "Did you just growl, beautiful witch mate?"

Maybe. She had meant that to be inside her own head, to psyche herself up. It had worked. "Yes, I did."

Titian kicked at a rock. "I hope she does. Remember what I said. In case she can't."

The brothers stayed silent. Kady did too.

She would save Black. She had to.

Kady swallowed down the fear. "You soldier boys have any idea how we can find the TFO and where they might have taken Black's soul?"

"Yes," the twins said in unison. Dunn grabbed Kady's arm and dragged her toward the ship.

Russ guided Black behind them.

"You're damn brazen flying around in a spaceship, aren't you boys?" Selena kicked at the bottom of the ship like she was kicking tires on a truck.

Titian crossed his arms and grinned. "Electra will kick your asses."

Russ ignored Titian all together and addressed Selena. "We learned a lot reconnoitering in the town called Three Mile Island. The people of this area have long been privy to advanced alien life, and our modes of transportation."

Niko snort-laughed. "The people of Rogue are used to just about anything and will keep quiet. But when you get outside of Bay county, you'd better disguise yourselves. I won't have you bears from outer space revealing the residents of my town to the world. This is a safe haven."

Russet looked at Niko like he was an idiot. "Duh. We have holographic projectors. Your people think we are something we found in your historical records called an excellent cycle around the sun blimp.

"Do you mean the Good Year blimp?" That was a conversation for another day. "Where are we going then?"

"There is an abandoned nuclear power plant called Three Mile Island. The TFO and the spectrals are there."

"Ha. I knew it," Selena pointed finger pistols, shooting off little sparks of magic in her glee, "That whole nuclear meltdown thing was a hoax to hide aliens."

Zara touched Kady's arm. "Be careful. We've had run-ins with these black government types."

"Thank you," Kady put her hand over Zara's, so grateful to have met a strong woman, who was also magical, and who she already thought of as a friend. A new thing for Kady. "But I have to go."

Zara nodded, and Niko came up behind her, wrapping his arms around her. "I know. I get it. More than you know. Go, save your mate, and when you're safe, come to Rogue. We'll take care of him at Doc's clinic and will be waiting for you."

"Hey, take Herbie with you, ya might need him." Selena placed Herbie, in broom form in her hand. "We'll watch after Percy for you."

Percy didn't like that idea at all. "I can help. I'll get a .44 Magnum and those TFO guys can make my day."

Kady took Percy aside. He'd been her friend for a long, long time, and she needed him to be that and so much more for her now. "Perc, I don't know what's going to happen tonight, and I'm scared. I'm doing my best to pretend I'm not, but I am."

"Even more reason I should go with you."

"Everything you said today, about who I am, and who I was meant to be... well, I don't think I would have believed, or even listened to anyone else besides you." Kady was asking a hard thing from a man who'd been a hedgehog as long as she'd known him. She didn't have anyone else, and it was her own fault.

If she made it through tonight, she'd have Black too, and the amazing people from Rogue, New York.

It was a start to building a life, one where she didn't hide anymore. She'd denied herself meaningful connections her entire life, scared of who she was, trying to protect her heart from another beat down. She hoped Percy understood.

She took his hand, so soft and smooth like his little hedgehog belly. "Which is why I need you to stay."

Percy stood little bit taller. "You need me to be Bill Munny."

"Yeah, because if I don't come back, I need you to make those TFO bad guys Unforgiven."

"I will, Kaden. Well, I guess they have it comin'. Anybody who don't wanna get killed better head on out the back."

She kissed his cheek. "Thank you."

Russet signaled to her to board the ship. "Niko and Doc have agreed to stay and be the clean-up team."

Niko glared at Russet, and Kady doubted "agree" was the right word. They boarded the ship and right before the door closed, a broom swooped in.

Kady grabbed it mid-air and the force of its forward momentum pushed her back and plopped her down on a bench attached to the interior wall of the ship.

The wood grain of his handle shimmered and transformed to match the metal of the walls around her. His bristles turned black and swirled like a tiny black hole. Kady reached out to touch it, but when her hand got close a sparkling blue shield zapped her finger.

"Whoa." Dunn examined Herbie. "Your broom is a miniature replica of our singularity drive. How did you do that?"

She shrugged. "I didn't. Herbie did."

"Who is Herbie?"

She held the shiny new Herbie up and at the same time, the spaceship lifted into the air. That had to be a coincidence.

Dunn didn't seem to notice. "I gotta get me a Herbie. He should come in handy on this op. Titian will be point, so follow his lead. He's sneaky as a fox in a hen house."

They accelerated, but Kady hardly felt the movement. She wouldn't have known if she couldn't see out the front. A few days ago, her only knowledge of spaceships were the Millennium Falcon, the Enterprise, and the Serenity. Now she was in one, on the way to rescue her soul mate with her magic. It was every geek-girl's dream.

This was no dream. Kady was scared. She swallowed and

tried to adopt the same get-shit-done attitude of the Star Marines around her. It didn't work, but she tried.

Titian pulled a vest and some weaponry looking gear out of a locker. "I heard that, you fucker. You only wish you could get into all the hen houses I do."

"Do you guys even know what a hen house is?"

All three of them gave her that look guys get when you ask them if they watch porn.

Russet sat at the controls of the ship and punched at buttons. "We've made contact with Fedelis inside the base. ETA seven minutes to his location."

God, that didn't give her much time. Maybe she had the ability to slow down time? That would be awesome.

She closed her eyes and concentrated, asking the Universe to help. Someone sat on the bench next to her.

"You look like you're going to throw up." Dunn's voice was gentle.

She wondered for a second about who his mate would be. A lucky guy or girl. Not as lucky as Kady, but still, Dunn had an air of calming grace. An alpha male who knew exactly who he was and what he wanted, no need to be a dick about it. She liked that about him.

She kept her eyes closed and absorbed that energy from him. "I might. Then I could spew all over the men in black. That would stop them in their tracks."

"You know, If you hadn't been matched to Black, our soul embers might have shined for you. You're quite a woman, Kady."

She popped her eyes open and stared at Dunn. So many things swirled in her mind. She should say thank you, she should ask about the plan, and she sure as shinola should ask if he meant what she thought he did with 'our soul embers.' The one question she cared about the answer to popped out. "What happens if we can't get his soul back?"

"You will, little warrior witch."

"What if that isn't our fate, Black's and mine? What if we're those star-crossed lovers who are meant for the tragedy and not the romance?"

"The Fates are twisted, so screw them. Make your own fate." He winked at her.

The ship landed behind an old tin building and the door swished open. The guys all stood, Dunn extending his hand to her.

Never had she wanted to run and hide more in her entire life. For the first time ever, she wouldn't do that. She'd fight for what she wanted and deserved.

She took a deep breath, gathering herself and the soul of her magic into the fierce warrior she was fated to be. "Fate or not, I'm ready."

"Fuck the Fates," Titian said, "let's go get your mate."

19

THE POWER IS IN YOU

Kady had her hand on Titian's shoulder. He led her around the side of the metal hangar building. Russet and Dunn sandwiched her in from behind. They had goggles on, techy guns raised, and grim faces that were so focused she actually felt safe.

None of them said a word, communicating only in hand signals. When Titian jogged, she jogged, when he crouched, she crouched, and promised herself to start doing yoga, Pilates, and Kung-Fu when this was all over.

Titian glanced back at her from their hiding spot behind an open door. He jerked his chin and indicated with two fingers toward a filing cabinet.

She looked but didn't see anything. Dunn popped his goggles off and placed them over her eyes. A full grown lion, big ole mane and everything, crouched next to the filing cabinet.

"Crikies," she whispered.

Dunn pressed his lips to her ear and said, "Fedelis."

As if that explained anything.

Titian moved their group across the darkened hanger to meet up with the lion. When they got there, the lion shoved the filing cabinet aside with its hip, revealing a trapdoor, not a whole lot wider than her butt.

"Black is down there?"

Dunn covered her mouth with his fingers, shushing her.

Fedelis dropped into the hole, sliding down a ladder, all sexy fireman style. Kady was no fireman. She stepped on the ladder and went down one rung, then two. They'd never get to Black's soul at this rate.

She took a deep breath, channeled the spirit of She-ra, Wonder Woman, and Princess Leia and jumped.

She landed right on her ass on a concrete floor about six feet down. Ouch. That was going to bruise.

Fedelis lay sprawled on the floor a few feet away, breathing, but unconscious. Oh, no. Had his soul been stolen?

"Russet, Dunn, hel—" Before she finished screaming for Black's brothers the trap door slammed shut and she heard the sound of weapons being fired.

"Hello, witch."

Agent Douchecanoe stood across from her in a weird space that was half maintenance room and half cave. She expected a Snidely Whiplash evil laugh from him, but he stepped out of the darkness and stared her down.

"You saved me a lot of time and energy coming to me."

Several spectral warriors hovered around him, but none of them were the right one. The hatred and animosity flowed from them, filling the room. Only her light inside kept her from buckling under the darkness.

She stood, rubbed the dirt off her pants, trying to stall while she came up with a plan. "Yeah, I didn't do it for you. Where's Black?"

"There is no Black, unless you mean his now black soul."

That she would never believe. "His soul is beautiful and strong and mine."

Agent Douchecanoe flung his arm, pointing to her and a wave of spectral warriors screeched and flew toward her, but not fast like before. They weren't there for her soul.

She threw up her shield, pushing it out to a good yard around her, encompassing Titian too. The asshole stared at where she'd been, invisible to him now.

She had maybe ten seconds before he figured out she hadn't moved. Her magic had thrown Russet and Dunn to the ground when she'd blasted them in the canyon, but they hadn't been hurt.

The spectrals barraged her shield, tearing at it, each time losing a limb to its effects. So many attacking all at the same time felt like she was being punched with spiky brass knuckles.

She brought balls of soul powered light into each of her hands, planning to fend them off. If she flung them now, they would evade like they had before. What else could she do?

A spark of a plan formed in her mind. She would need them to get much closer.

The agent approached her shield, still trying to see through it to her. "You and your kind are standing in the way of progress, witch."

Each bite of the spectrals to her shield decreased her power, but also their own. That power had to be going somewhere. "How is this progress, you asshat?"

Finally figuring out where she was, Agent Douchecanoe strode across the room like he owned it. Maybe he did. He wasn't scared of her even a little bit with the spectrals at his beck and call. Their scratching and clawing at her shield grew harder, hurting her deeper.

"The spectral warriors will allow us to have dominance in the galaxy. We will be able to control the resources and the people. We may be behind in the space race in technology, but we won't be for long."

He reached out and touched the shimmering wall of her shield. His fingers skimmed it and Kady felt something different. Something she could harness.

"We've made a few connections since the first aliens landed at Roswell, ones that will help us eliminate these damn Space Marines. America will become the superpower in space that it is here on Earth."

Oh. My. Gerrrrd. What a dumbass. A dumbass with a soul. Even if he didn't know how to use it properly. But she did. She reduced her shield's range to have the space, drawing the spectrals in, hoping the agent would follow. They did and redoubled their attacks. Scratches filled with blood appeared on her arms and neck. They stung, and she almost pushed them all back again.

She had to get them closer though. Centimeter by centimeter she drew them all in, talking too as a distraction both to them and herself.

"Are you for real? You're doing this for America? There's a whole entire Universe out there."

That's it, a little bit closer. She could feel the light of his soul, scarily dim. But there was some. With each inch they gained, the burns to her skin intensified. Much more and she'd be on fire.

"Don't be stupid, the Universe has always been there, but with the alliances we've made, now it's ours for the taking."

How did one make alliances with hatred and evil? Probably why this guy's soul was so dim. A little more. Please, Universe, don't let her collapse before they got to her.

"Either you're with us, or you're against us, witch. I've seen what your powers can do, how you can interact with the spectral force. Join Task Force Omega, and you'll be a key player in keeping America strong."

His soul wasn't enough. She needed more. The only one she'd ever drawn on was Black's. Agent Douchecanoe's felt slightly slimy and was hard for her to work with.

The spectrals' souls floating around her, beating at her, had no light. She couldn't get anything but pain and despair from them.

She examined the horrible beings looking for one in particular. Titian's wasn't there. Which meant he was still alive with an intact soul.

"I don't think so. You're a bully, your agency is a bully. I don't like bullies."

He pulled something out of his pocket and clasped it in his hand. "I like that. Bully. Suits me."

She reached out and found a soul that was soft like silk, almost slippery, but that burned hot and bright.

Yes. Kady threw gratitude out into the universe and drew Fedelis's soul out in swirls of tawny gold.

The balls of light in her hands grew bright, then faltered for a moment. A slash cut through the shield, hitting her right over her heart. One more hit like that, and she was toast.

"You're the stupid one if you think you can control the spectrals without losing your own soul.

He laughed like she'd just told the most hilarious joke ever. "I don't control the Spectrals. Someone else does that. She could use your help. Your powers are too valuable for us not to possess."

It was now, or never.

"Your spectrals, and your boss can kiss my curvy ass. I'm getting my mate back." Kady dropped her shield and drug all the power and light around the spectrals. The orbs she created were slow to move, but they bubbled through the air and divided. She encased one spectral while another lashed out at her, knocking her to her knees.

She reached inside, to the place no one, not even Black had ever touched. It was the place she kept the truest part of herself, the one that wanted to be a warrior and a lover and shining light for the world.

Kady tapped into that most authentic piece of her soul and added its power to this battle.

She was a warrior.

Each spectral was sucked into a bubble of light. Their shadows shrunk, cowering and faded to nothing more than the shadow of a rat.

Agent Douchecanoe recoiled and stumbled, first putting

his hand over his heart, staring at the dark green swirls coming off his skin.

"What are you doing to me, you bitch?" He held his clasped hand out and Black's soul ember dropped and dangled. It glowed like a star in the sky.

Kady reached out for it. That was hers and this guy was defiling it just by touching it.

He grasped the pendant in his hand and closed his eyes. Sweat beaded on his forehead and Black's spectral warrior rose beside him, vibrating with hatred and dark power.

"Black." A terrible sadness rushed over Kady, smashing against her, dragging her own soul into darkness.

Agent Douchecanoe thrust his fist forward and the spectral warrior that was Black charged at her, screaming louder the closer it got.

The bitter taste of fear blistered the back of her throat. She pushed it down and closed her eyes. She called up that power inside, the part that was the lover, that the soul of her true love brought to the surface.

She wrapped the charging warrior in a field of it, stopping him mere centimeters from her.

"Black, are you in there? Can you hear me?"

It screamed and screeched, lashing out at her. So much pain prickled across their connection that it stole her breath away.

"Fool, it can't understand you, they are stupid barely conscious bastards."

Kady shot her hand out, releasing one of the spectrals. It charged the agent and engulfed him. His gray green soul rose from his chest and his body dropped to the floor. The spectral didn't relent, continuing to scratch and pull and bite until a fine dusting of ash was all that was left of Agent Douchecanoe and his soul.

Before she could envelop the remaining spectral warrior, it streaked past her and through the rock wall of the cave, disappearing.

The cord and pendant that contained Black's soul ember sat on the ground next to the ash. Kady crawled across the floor and picked it up. The golden fire inside was the most beautiful thing she'd ever seen.

She slipped the cord around her neck. The pendant fell between her breasts, resting over her heart. A warmth like a fire on a cold winter's night pooled inside of her and her skin glowed with light and heat.

The trapped spectrals shrieked, cowering from her light.

All except one.

Black's spectral warrior stared transfixed on her and the light emanating from her, lighting up the room.

The words of a spell whispered into her mind. She held the pendant in her open hand.

"I am yours and you are mine. Together, forever, will we shine. The ember of your soul, over my heart will lay. Come and be with me now, in your heart I will stay."

Black's soul pulsed with a luminescence, fluctuating from an empty dark absence of light, to purple, then blue, green, to yellow, then back to the rich golden tones that matched his skin. She pulled him into the pendant, barely containing all the light inside.

"Kady?" Titian propped himself up on and elbow and looked around at the fiery orbs of light containing the remains of the spectrals. "Fucking hell, woman. Is that my soul magic?"

She nodded. The orbs swirled and the orange light that was the part of his soul she'd borrowed for the battle danced and jumped across the room and back into Titian's body.

The form of his lion shimmered and then receded. "Fates above. Glad you're on our team."

"I have his soul, Fedelis. Can you move? We need to get to Black."

"Yeah, I can, but how is the question. We aren't going back out the same way we came in." He stood and pointed to the tunnel they'd dropped down. The metal was mangled and, in some parts, melted to the side of the wall.

"I don't remember doing that."

"No, that's the effects of a pulse grenade. Looks like the Barrett boys had quite a battle while we were down here. I don't know what we'll find up top."

A rumble began on one side of the cave and rocks fell from the ceiling. Fedelis grabbed her and pulled her back. "Take cover."

They ducked and crouched next to the nearest wall, and the room shattered. Light streamed in from the outside and a full-size tank crashed into the room.

Russet and Dunn stood on the sides, weapons at the ready. Titian looking exactly like the fox who'd just broken into the henhouse rode on top.

"Nice timing dickheads. Kady already saved the day. Where the fuck did you get a tank?"

Russet jumped down and rushed to Kady's side. "Did you find Black?"

She nodded and smiled, grasping the ember in her hand.

"Then let's get you to Rogue. Herbie?"

In a blink, Kady's old red and white pickup truck appeared where the tank had been. The guys dropped down into the truck bed.

"I seriously have got to get me a Herbie," Dunn said shaking his head.

"What about those guys?" Titian asked, indicating over his shoulder with his thumb, pointing toward the trapped specks of spectrals.

"I'm pretty sure those cages will hold them until we are away. I can't hold them forever, but long enough."

Kady climbed into the front seat and didn't even have to turn the ignition. Herbie took them out to the hangar and parked next to the bear's ship.

They were all safely inside and airborne again within moments. They couldn't get to Rogue fast enough for Kady. The hilly land and scrub brush flew by in a blur. They crossed a small lake and a river where she swore she saw a couple of dragons. They must be close.

The was nothing on the horizon, then in an instant, the town appeared. Russet came in for a landing several hundred yards from the nearest building.

Black waited for her, standing at the edge of town. Zara and Niko were by his side.

Kady pushed at the door controls, sliding them open before the ship touched down. The wind blew her hair and she hit the ground running, needing to be with Black as soon as she could.

Herbie, in his spaceship broom form swooped her up and

dropped her a few feet away from him. She stood there for a few breaths. What if this didn't work?

She had his soul, but could she get it back inside of his body, and would he be the same man she'd fallen in love with?

"Good luck," Zara whispered. She grabbed Niko's hand and stepped away.

"Black." He looked at her, like a child or a puppy when its name is called. "Lower your head, let me slip this around your neck."

He did as he was told and Kady placed the pendant over his head. She helped him to stand up straight again and prayed for his soul to reunite with his body.

Nothing happened.

"Please universe, please put my heart back together again." Kady placed her hand over Black's heart, pressing the ember into his skin. It glowed beneath her hand, but nothing more.

"Black," she whispered, "you listen to me, now. I was lost and alone until you crashed into me. You helped me find the power living inside of me. I know it's there without you coaxing it up with your kisses and your love, but I want to share it with you."

Had the ember grown brighter or was it only Kady's own magic, or wishful thinking?

"Come back to me, Black. Share my life, be my love, I'll give you my soul in return. Come back to me."

She pulled Black's head down to hers, touching her forehead to his, then a kiss to his lips.

He was soft and warm, then the place where they

touched grew hot, tingling, burning, scorching, but not in pain, but in pleasure.

Black wrapped his arms around her, pushing his tongue into her mouth, sucking at her lips, pulling at her soul.

"Kady?" he whispered her name.

Nothing had ever sounded as joyful and sweet.

20

MARKED FOREVER

The Gundersons had set up their tiny house containers in a circle at the end of one of Rogue's streets near the edge of the Reserve. Margreth had already planted flowers and trees, recreating the garden they'd left behind.

They gifted the house that looked like the land and sky to Black and Kady upon their triumphant return.

A permanent rainbow shined in the sky above where Black stood, and he couldn't care less about any of it.

The only beauty he could see was the light and the love shining in Kady's eyes. He never wanted to be without his warrior witch again. He wouldn't be if he could help it.

There was a black place inside his soul that he'd never acknowledged before, but he'd lived there, in the dark and it couldn't be ignored.

The only thing that made him forget was having Kady in his arms. They'd fallen asleep together before they could make love, but Black had awakened, restless.

He came outside to stare up and the night sky. The stars and the arm of the galaxy the Earthers called the Milky Way reminded him of nights on Honaw.

The view wasn't quite the same, but close, and that soothed him. He longed to go home to Honaw's craggy mountains and untamed forests.

But how could he with everything that had happened?

"Black?"

Kady came out of the little house, wrapped in only a light blanket. It barely concealed her lush hips and ripe breasts. The sight of her stirred a longing and desire in him so deep for a moment it pushed away the darkness in his soul.

The pendant, the sliver of his soul hanging around his neck lit up, shining its light on her. Her own golden glow responded, swirling around her.

"*Mah wah*, come let me wrap my arms around you and enjoy the beauty of the night with me."

Maybe he would never return to Honaw, or be able to show Kady his home, but they could make a life together here in Rogue. He could be a farmer like his mother, forget about battles and war.

Would Kady understand the sacrifice they both would be giving when he went back into space to fight again?

He hugged her close and stared up and the stars. "I understand the spectrals now in a way that no one has before."

She snuggled into him. "Yes. I can feel the difference in you."

He couldn't look at her yet. He needed her to understand. "For the first time, I think we've got a shot and beating them."

She touched his face, not looking at the sky at all, but up at him. "That's good, isn't it?"

The love in his heart overflowed, but he tempered it. "Yes. But, Kady, my heart, my soul, I don't know what to do. How do I go back into battle and leave you behind?"

She smiled and pulled him down for a kiss. Her touch was fire and it beat back the coldness he'd been wrapped in. He lingered on her lips, wanting to touch and taste her forever.

She was the one who broke their kiss. "You don't, silly bear. You will be with me and defeat those monsters. Because we will do it together."

Yes. The power and truth of her words crashed over him reinvigorating his soul. He only had a vague sense of what had happened in the battle for his soul, but the one part he understood was that Kady's power, her magic, her light inside had drawn him out of the darkness.

"Together we will be stronger than anyone else who can battle the spectrals." He didn't have to win this war on his own.

"Yes, we will. But tomorrow. Tonight, you are mine."

He would make love to her and their souls would dance together in the light. But first he had a question he'd been wanting to ask her since the day they'd met.

"Kady, on my homeworld, when two souls are joined in marriage, we have a celebration with our friends and family."

"A wedding?"

"Yes, do you have this on Earth?"

"Yeah." She bit her lip and that lovely flush he so adored rose to her cheeks.

"My brothers are here already, but can we contact your family, ask them to come?"

She shook her head. "Until yesterday I didn't have family. Percy told me about who I came from, but that my parents are dead."

He hadn't known she was a bear descendant until the witch Selena had called her Kaden Ayininkizi. "I'm sorry, love. Wait, did you say Percy told you? Isn't that your hedgehog?"

She giggled. "I forgot you don't know. He turned into a pretty handsome guy."

Should he be worried? Naw. A bear-shifter trumped a hedgehog, right? "What else did he say?"

"Turns out I'm descended from bears and witches, and I have sisters. Maybe, if you're asking what I think you're asking, we could find them?"

Oh, he was asking. Right now.

"Yes, *mah wah*. We can." He took a step back, asked the Fates for their blessing and lifted Kady into his arms. "Kaden Ayininkizi, Warrior Bear's Daughter. Will you wear my soul ember and be my mate for all eternity?" He slipped the pendant from around his neck, finally able to properly give her his soul.

"Yes, oh yes, Black." She dipped her head and let him place his ember around her neck. It dangled over her heart, flashed bright like a supernova, and settled into a warm golden glow.

She dropped the blanket on the ground and awed him with her beauty. There were very few things in the Universe more desirable than a woman in love who was confident and strong.

"Black, make me yours."

With pleasure.

He took her lips in a kiss that sealed their fates together. Her tongue met his, playful and sweet. He laid Kady down on the blanket wanting to kiss every centimeter of her. A cool breeze blew across their bodies and her nipples tightened. They looked so inviting he decided to start there.

He licked one and sucked it into his mouth, tasting her again as if for the first time.

"Mmm. I love when you do that." She threaded her fingers into his hair holding him to her breast. Her soft golden light flickered across her skin.

His own light responded in kind.

He found her other nipple with his hand and pinched at her taut skin, tugging and playing until she squirmed beneath him.

He needed her hot and wanting because his own body was on fire for her, and once he was inside her, there would be no stopping the claiming this time.

She wore his ember, she was a part of his soul. Tonight, she would bare his mark, tonight and forever more.

He gave her other nipple a quick kiss and worked his way down her body. First, the soft underside of her breasts, then the gentle swell of her belly.

He dipped his tongue into her belly button and stayed an extra moment savoring the skin over her womb.

Someday soon, after they'd won their war, he would put a baby in her belly. They would raise a half dozen cubs and surround them both with the solid foundation of family.

Two more kisses down and he spread her thighs. Her curls were already wet, and he wanted nothing more than to hear her call his name as he licked and sucked her clit.

"Black, stop teasing me with your hot breath. Please take me, taste me. I need your mouth on me."

"You're in for some teasing now." He licked up one pussy lip and down the other, going nowhere near her clit just yet.

He slid a finger inside of her and she arched her back, trying to take more. He added a second finger and sunk into her wet heat. She moaned, and his cock twitched, loving the sound of her pleasure.

The first rays of her light streaked toward the sky. They had no fear she would draw the spectrals with her power here. The town of Rogue was protected, thanks to Zara, Selena and the other witches.

That was a good thing, because Black intended on crating one hell of a fireworks show in the Gundersons' new garden.

He crooked his fingers inside Kady and found just the right spot. A few swipes and she was panting. "That's it, baby, ride my fingers."

"I need more, Black. More."

He licked the fingers on his other hand and slid them down until he found that sweet pucker. He circled and teased, until she whimpered his name.

"Please, Black."

He loved she wanted him in every way. "I'll take you in every way tonight, *mah wah*."

"Yes, yes. Now, my love."

He bent his head, finding her clit and licking it up and down. Her legs trembled. She was close, and he wanted to push her over the edge. He pressed the tip of his finger into her anus, licked her clit, and slid his other hand in and out of her pussy.

Her light sparkled, and she cried out his name on repeat. "Black, Black, Black."

When the tight ring of muscle relaxed, he pushed in further, matching the thrusts of his fingers with the licks across her clit.

Kady's body locked, then exploded around him. Her clit pulsed in his mouth, her pussy clamped around his hand, and her ass throbbed, milking his finger.

Her orgasm sucked at his own soul, drawing him into her pleasure. She was so damn amazing. How had he gotten so lucky with the Fates to have her as a mate?

He didn't stop pressing her body for more, drawing her orgasm out for as long as he could.

Her legs finally collapsed, and her body went slack. He loved seeing the satisfaction written across her face and skin.

He withdrew and kissed his way back up her body, stopping to notice each flush. "I love making you come, Kady. Your body is so responsive, so perfect in every way. How do you feel?"

"Fine and dandy, thank you very much." She was still breathing hard and her eyes were closed.

"Let me see the sparkle in your eyes."

She got an adorable lopsided grin and blinked up at him

through her lashes. Beautiful. "Hey, how are you still wearing clothes and I'm out here naked as the day is long?"

"I'll happily fix that."

"Allow me." She wrinkled her nose, wiggling it, and his clothes disappeared.

"I love doing that."

"I kind of like that particular spell, myself." He kissed and cuddled her, stroking over all her soft skin until she was aroused again.

"Black, I need something from you," she instinctively rubbed her hand across her shoulder, "but I don't know what it is."

Black knew. He'd waited far to long to give this part of himself to her. "The mark, sweet witch of mine. This time when I make love to you, I will mark you with my bite and the whole universe will know you are mine."

Her eyes lit up, instantly understanding and wanting her own need for the marking fulfilled.

"God, yes. Make love to me, Black. Mark me, make me yours." Kady kissed him, licking and biting at his lips.

Now that she knew of the marking and wore his ember her need increased. It would only be satisfied when he was inside of her thrusting and biting her neck.

Only then would he too be satisfied.

Black spread Kady's legs again and wrapped them over his arms. That raised her ass off the ground and gave him the perfect angle to sink his cock deep into her.

He notched the sensitive head of his cock just inside her entrance. It felt unbelievable and if he didn't know it would get even better, he'd stay right there like this, staring into Kady's eyes until morning.

"Kady, *mah wah*, my warrior beauty. I love you with all my soul."

Their light shone all around them, sparking through the air, swirling and dancing together.

"I love you, Black. More than I ever thought possible. I love you."

Black thrust into her body, as deep as he could. They fit together so perfectly. He withdrew halfway and thrust in again. Their bodies became light and fire, the flames dancing to the rhythm of their lovemaking.

They would make love more times than he could count, but he would remember tonight for as long as they both shall live.

Kady stared into his eyes and grasped his face in her hands making sure he could see every flash, every glint, every ember of her love.

Their pulses pounded, their breathing synced, their heartbeats met and matched. Their bodies became one.

The dance of light above them, their souls danced together, swirling together with each thrust into her, each time she pushed her body to meet his, until there was no distinction between his light and hers. Their souls were one, never to be broken apart, together for all time.

"Together, forever, my love." Kady's pussy fluttered and tightened around his cock, and her nipples beaded. She was on the verge of coming and so was he.

He broke her gaze and kissed her. Then he lowered his

mouth to the soft spot between her neck and shoulder. On his next thrust he bit down, hard enough to mark her, but not enough to break the skin. He poured his soul into hers imbuing the bite with his intentions. He claimed her for himself for all time.

Kady cried out, not in pain, but the pleasure they both felt at finally truly mating and belonging to each other. Her cliNiko swept through her body, their light exploded into the sky. Black went with her, giving her his essence and his soul, coming so deep inside of her that he never wanted to be anywhere else.

Together.

Forever.

They floated in their bliss for as long as they could. It was a beautiful place and it would be their refuge in the hard times ahead.

"I love you, you big alien bear of mine. You're amazing and I can't wait to spend the rest of my life with you."

"Ah, my beautiful curvy witch. I cursed the Fates the day they crashed me into this crazy blue planet, but I'll thank them the rest of my life for you and your love. I love you, *mah wah*."

A touch of Fate had brought Kady into his life, and now that he had her, he would never let her go.

Want to read the Dragon Warrior version of this story? Check out Tamed: The Black Dragon Brotherhood book one.

Interested in reading the Troika wolf pack's stories? Start with Dirty Wolf: Alpha Wolves Want Curves book one.

Need more curvy heroines and the hot guys who love them? Sign up for the Curvy Connection newsletter and I'll send you a free curvy girl romance book right away!

A LETTER FROM THE AUTHOR

Dear Reader,

I had so much fun playing in an alternate universe to my dragons' world. I am a sci-fi geeky girl at heart. (I've always had a thing for stormtroopers. lol) There's a lot of the real me in Kady so I hope you found something in her journey you could relate to too.

If you loved Black and Kady's story and would like more curvy women to see that there are stories out there for them too, would you leave a review for this book?

Even one line that says: Loved this book, or Hooray for curvy girl romance books, or even Good Job, Aidy – would make my day (and you'd be helping more readers find the book!)

As each book of the Black Dragon Brotherhood comes out, I'll release the Fated for Curves alternate universe book to match.

Want to know what happens next in the Fated for Curves series?

Let's ask the Fates!

Hmm... they're giggling and saying something about a set of bearded bear-shifter twins and how their mate is going to drive them crazy.

Sounds like fun ~ Check out *A Tangled Fate* at *aidyaward.com/fated-for-curves*.

Hugs,
--Aidy

ALSO BY AIDY AWARD

The Black Dragon Brotherhood

Tamed

Tangled

Fated For Curves

Touch of Fate

Dragons Love Curves

Chase Me

Tease Me

Unmask Me

Bite Me

Cage Me

Baby Me

Defy Me

Surprise Me

Dirty Dragon

Crave Me

Slay Me

Alpha Wolves Want Curves

Dirty Wolf

Naughty Wolf

Kinky Wolf

The Curvy Love Series

Curvy Diversion

Curvy Temptation

Curvy Persuasion

The Curvy Seduction Saga

Rebound

Rebellion

Reignite

ABOUT THE AUTHOR

Aidy Award is a curvy girl who kind of has a thing for stormtroopers. She's also the author of the popular Curvy Love series and the hot new Dragons Love Curves series. She writes curvy girl erotic romance, about real love, and dirty fun, with happy ever afters because every woman deserves great sex and even better romance, no matter her size, shape, or what the scale says.

Read the delicious tales of hot heroes and curvy heroines come to life under the covers and between the pages of Aidy's books. Then let her know because she really does want to hear from her readers.

Connect with Aidy on her website. www.AidyAward.com get her Curvy Connection, and join her Facebook Group - Aidy's Amazeballs.

Made in the USA
Columbia, SC
27 September 2020